Ghost Soldiers

Ghost Soldiers

A Novel of the Vietnam War
Revised Edition

Steven Hardesty

STEVENS & MARLIN PUBLISHING, LLC

SARASOTA, FLORIDA

25th Anniversary Edition (Revised)

Steven Hardesty
Stevens & Marlin Publishing, LLC
PO Box 4006
Sarasota, Florida, 34230 USA

www.stevenhardesty.com
www.stevensandmarlinbooks.com

Cover design by James at goonwrite.com
Cover image by Shutterstock
Book Layout © 2013 BookDesignTemplates.com

Ghost Soldiers/Steven Hardesty —2d edition (revised)
ISBN 9781717748768
20170328/20180717

Preface to the Revised Edition

This is the story of the soldier's dream of victory and survival in the miseries of war and of his use of fantasy to endure hardship and despair. Part of the story is reality. Part is fantasy. Put those things together and, when you have read the last page, you will know what it was like inside the head of a ground soldier in the Vietnam war.

However, as I heard from readers – and particularly veterans – about this novel since it was first published in 1986, I realized the book needed sharpening to better tell a story that means a great deal to me. This text includes those changes.

But this book has one more purpose. The old hymn says "Once to every man and nation comes the moment to decide." When that moment comes to you as citizen or soldier to help this country decide once again for peace or war, I hope this story gives you some of what you need to make your choice.

Steven Hardesty
August 16, 2011

At the beginning

Protected by infantry, by gun cars and helicopters, truck convoys ground up the two asphalt lanes of Highway 19 and wound quickly through the hills of the Vietnamese coastal province, away from the beaches and jungle heat, up onto the cool plateau of the Central Highlands. The convoys cut west through corn country, lettuce country, bean country, across chalky Deo Mang Pass and into the core of Binh Dinh Province, into the city of An Khe under the gaze of the jungle warriors of five armies.

In An Khe the convoys delivered rifles, rifles designed for American arm-lengths and American finger-sizes, rifles intended for the American soldiers squatting in their highland camps waiting for the war to end. Then the relentless convoys ground on over Bridge 25, into Mang Yang Pass, past the graves of a thousand French legionnaires, and across the dusty plateau carrying their rifles to other cities and other soldiers.

In the armories of the great American base at An Khe lay new rifles, small, black M-16 rifles. Weapons that with the flip of a switch could become light machineguns. The men of the five armies of the Highlands — Yanks, Arvins, Koreans, Chucks and North Viets — ignored these rifles as they ignored the mechanics of war that had brought them because they *lived in reveries of the war's imminent end. They were deceived, the mechanics of war deceived them.*

To the commanders of the American basecamp it seemed pointless to continue issuing American rifles to American soldiers when the war, so nearly over, was intended to train and equip the South Vietnamese, so the new rifles were distributed to Arvin soldiers, instead. These soldiers sold their rifles to the Chucks or to the Korean soldiers for seventy-five dollars apiece. Their families driven to starvation by the war needed the money. A few Koreans resold the rifles for two hundred dollars apiece to the American soldiers who were helpless without good rifles. Normal troop rotation caused most of these bought-back rifles to be sent with their Yank owners into the highlands forests and jungles, where the soldiers of five armies dreamed of the war's end. The rifles — the product of a simple mechanic of war — renewed the killing, and the war did not end.

Part I

1.

Zap

Who was he to be asleep now, when everything that was about to happen already was on its way to him? He was a soldier who was never going to be issued an American rifle. The U.S. Army gave him one each: pistol, automatic, .45, and eight each: rounds, .45, and one each: magazine, .45. That was supposed to see him through the war and get him home alive. He slept naked and sweating on his cot, in dog tags and boots, under the mosquito net, his black hair thrown out on the pillow, his hand flung down to the floor, dreaming of the rifle he could never have to keep himself alive.

He was Waldo – Second Lieutenant, Headquarters Battery, 1st Battalion, 2nd Field Artillery Regiment – but to the men monitoring the Fire Direction Control radio net, tracking him through forest and jungle, across swamps, through the vills, with the infantry, he was call sign Yonkers two-four. Yonkers two-four who had no rifle. He was a young man of middling height and, before the war, of middling character. Now he was something different. The howl and roar of the news was on its way to him. But he was asleep.

Zap

Others were awake in that night, velvet black and thick, filled with tropic steam and the smell of candles burning in the fog sliding down the mountainslopes, Orion swinging in the sky above Old Baldy and its twin, Hill 415. A young and frightened soldier watching from a sandbagged bunker on lonely Bridge 25 was awake. He spotted the flashing red lights of a shot-up helicopter spinning down behind the saddleback and reached for the landline. "Wake up!" he shouted.

Zap

Staff Sergeant Mars was awake in basecamp, sitting at the N.C.O. Club bar with his bottle. He had a drooping gray handlebar mustache and a baldness so perfect his head looked like a giant thumb. He held curious prejudices for a soldier. He drank no coffee, ate no beef. He believed his enemies on the battlefields of the underdeveloped world were men starved of those commodities and so could smell them on his breath. In the field he bathed rarely and only with antiviral soaps that had no odor. He ate native foods and not the muck served in army C ration cans. His sweating dreams were of crawling Chucks with knives and eye-gouging awls but he did not sleep with his rifle as did others. He dreaded to be startled awake and shoot the wrong kind. Tonight, he was afraid to sleep – afraid to dream. Suddenly, he could not remember where he had set down his rifle. He stopped his drinking and sat there, waiting.

Zap

A tingling in the back of his skull – a death cry from machine to man – and Sergeant Mars like a man touched by the finger of God flung out his hands across the bar to grasp the planed ammo-case wood, knocking glasses and Scotch to the cement floor. His fellow noncoms cursed him and kicked the shards under the bar and shouted at the Vietnamese girls

6

for more booze. Mars – that really was his name – got off his bar stool and went banging through the club door, his company buck sergeants, Knobs and The Bee, bow-legged from being footsore, followed him on the run, their jungle boots slapping the cement floor while the bartender shouted for her money. "Sa'rn, where we goin'?" they cried.

Zap

Sergeant Mars stood in the officers' shack, walls of wood stripped from ammo crates and supported outside by rotting sandbags where rats hissed through the fly screens, and watched Waldo sleep. The radio played softly. He was naked but in laced boots, his body slashed by elephant grass, nicked, bruised, his black hair flung out on the sweat-stained pillow, one hand was spread across an oozing wound on his chest, the other arm stretched down to the floor, the hand under a bush hat. "Never seen a man sleep like that in basecamp," said Sergeant Knobs.

Mars stretched a hand toward the radio and slowly raised the volume. Waldo slowly uncurled from under his netting, the bush hat falling from his hand, and brought up to eye level the .45 pistol he had there, his thumb clicking off the safety, the two bucks wide-eyed, Mars saying, "It's Sergeant Mars, Lieutenant, it's me." Waldo came conscious. He dropped the pistol on the cot. Knobs and The Bee glanced at each other to say, This one's crazier than the rest of us.

"Chopper down," said Mars.

What? You finally pull three days' R-and-R after weeks humping the boonies and some bastard takes a fall. Where are his own kind to find him, that chopper kind? But Waldo dressed, slung his artillery net radio over his shoulder, the .45 on his hip, a pack of C rats on his back, compass on its boot lace at his neck, rubbing his hand over his sweat-glistening combat shave to rasp himself fully awake. It was as though he had never waked or never slept, his choices waking nightmare or the sleep of the dead. So tired. They ran to the rally point.

Zap

When Peepsite thought about it, which was something he rarely did in the middle of a night like this – soldiers can afford to think about nothing but war or they will die, he was convinced, especially in Chuckie's wild night – he believed that if he wasn't really there, they couldn't really kill him. It was a brilliant solution to the problem of how to survive the war. Much of the time he dreamed himself in college in a vast lecture hall crammed with eager fellow students listening to a fantastic lecture on the mating habits of white rats or the history of quick-frozen orange juice. For hours he would be content and safe in that lecture hall. Then the war would intrude and he would have to remind himself and everyone around him that he wasn't really there, or Chuckie was free to kill him.

Peepsite was not entirely satisfied with his solution as there were people — particularly the captain — who were prejudiced against it, and they were preventing him from making corporal. "Come back down to earth, Peeps," the captain would say, slapping Peepsite on the rump so hard Peeps spit out the bennies he was about to swallow. "Ya gotta cope, boy, ya gotta cope without them pills." Captain Oliver Foley would wiggle his big brows above the thick eyeglasses held to his face by a strap around his head under his bush hat and clop up the trail, adjusting his pack straps and shaking his big Missouri ass. "Are ya copin', boy?" he called back to Peepsite.

When Mars, Waldo, and the bucks found Peepsite, he was sprawled on an endless, imaginary green lawn covered with pines and ivied buildings, feeling up a coed excited by his twisted nose and uneven eyes which gave the impression he was made of two halves of two different men indifferently glued together.

"Chopper down, Peepsite," said Sergeant Mars.

"I ain't really here," said Peepsite in protest.

"I know you ain't. Let's go."

Zap

Captain Foley met them as he banged out the door of the dolly shack, his gear and weapons hanging from him in disarray. "Sar'n Mars, rouse the boys. Chopper down — just got the call from higher." He buckled his black gloves and they ran for the track park, men leaping from the shadow, strapping on gear, slamming home magazines, the armored personnel carriers grumbling like Mack trucks and spitting smoke, their gunners hooting for Bravo. This was Bravo Company, Captain Foley's company, forty-two men, a third of what was demanded in the field manuals, but this was Vietnam and no outfit was full strength. Then, neither was the enemy. Only the choppers and Sergeant Mars had all their magic in this war.

"Climb aboard — no time — chopper down!"

They crawled up the square sides of the aluminum boxes, pulling themselves up on the gunshields and grabbing the equipment tie-downs or bracing themselves against the .50 turret or the .30 machinegun shields. The tracks clacked forward out of the vehicle park, flashing their Red Elephant logos and their Dixie battle flags, down the asphalt road laid between fields of weed toward the glaring watchtower lights of the main gate. They jerked hard right, piling on speed, cowboys howling into the wind, following Mars in communion with the fallen chopper. They howled down the highway into Chuckie's jungle and Chuckie's night and Chuckie's pouring rain, the tracks bouncing over ruts and gullies, the G.I.s clinging to the machineguns, sliding over the wet decks, antennas and pennants cracking overhead, their fright and fury to fight building to rage as they whistled and chanted obscenities at Chuck's night.

They howled into V.C. Valley at forty miles an hour firing flares into the fields around the sandbag bunker where the boy stood who had seen the chopper fall. They shouted for entry onto Bridge 25, firing wildly with all guns into the dripping head-high elephant grass, streaks of good American orange tracer sizzling through Chuck's territory – the night – and

9

slicing up Chuck's fog sagging down the mountainsides. The young soldier who had seen the chopper fall swung back the wire barricade, pointed to the saddle between the two tree-covered mountains and said, "There!"

Now it begins

Sergeant Mars and Captain Daddy shouted the Bravos into the elephant grass where each couldn't see the man next to him and with Waldo they swept south, platoons-on-line, bucking back the tall, wet weed with their rifle stocks as they left behind the comfort of the tracks' big guns.

The Captain and Fruitcake took the point. Fruitcake was a gangly country boy whose fear gave him the grace of a light-stepping, long-legged spider when he was in the brush, and he could smell Chuck. He was a coward who knew no bushwhackers would risk alerting the company by blasting the point man. Despite his size and his strange spider-jumping down the trail, he figured to survive the war. He had dreams of winning a Bronze Star to go with his Combat Infantryman's Badge to show off back on the block, even though he knew only officers got the B.S. He might get it if he were dead, of course, and that presented him a problem.

As for Captain Foley — he took the point because it was his fantasy that he was a soldier when he was really a Missouri village parson. The army had proved a delightful surprise to him. In Missouri he was considered a woodsman barely competent to find his way across a parking lot. The army, however, was less demanding and cared not at all that he had once put his company on the wrong mountaintop when the army sent choppers to pull them out of Chuck's pincers — the army just sent the choppers from the right mountain to the wrong mountain and got them out anyway, and gave him a B.S. for bringing back forty-two living bods and six wounded-in-action, none killed. That was an achievement: He won no battles but he got no one killed. Who won battles, Foley wondered? No one, really. What was a battle? You stumble through the jungle or the pine forest, half-blind from bennies, from exhaustion, from too much patrolling or fright or sweat or rain or sun, and you find yourself standing in a mess of surprised Chucks and you shoot them and they shoot you and you stumble away dragging your wounded thinking, God, we skirted the pit one more time, and then you stumble into another nest of Chucks and it goes on and on. No one at higher cares that your men are exhausted, war-weary, too frightened to blow grass, too frightened to carry bourbon in their canteens like Sar'n Mars. The helis never come on time or when they do they mistake you for Chuck and shoot you up. You never have enough to eat. You shoot up your ammo and *then* Chuck wants to fight you. You stink. Your boots are torn on pungi stakes. Diarrhea runs down your legs. The leeches eat you at night. No water. The men fall out by the trail in shivering exhaustion and you take them in your arms. You search for their salt tabs but their canteens are empty. When the whole mix gets too much for them they go nuts and throw tear gas grenades at one another, laughing like idiots. No one at higher gives a damn. The battalion commander leaves in two weeks, he wants to go out in a blaze of glory and he really wants that Legion of Honor to pin on his chest, but he's never been out in the field – one of the lucky ones who got too old, too fat, too much rank between wars to have to fight in this one. What is he going to make me do?

Dead French legionnaires pricked at the corners of his eyes. Foley turned to stare. They were gone in muted *pops!* Their strange grim smiles lingered. "I'm a rat that's jumped too often," he said aloud.

Loping Fruitcake looked at his captain in surprise, then cursed him softly. He was concentrating on his hands and feet — dreaming he hadn't any. He was trying to decide which he could do without to win his B.S.

Waldo dropped out of a tree. He might as well have been out of the sky, he startled Fruitcake so badly. Fruitcake cursed again, louder, his reverie of sidewalk glory broken. He sulked ahead through the dripping weed, picking at his pimples, rain draining off his bush hat.

"Can't see any chopper flames nor a burn zone, Captain." Waldo clutched his radio mike. "Let me drop some flares. At least they'll know we're out here looking for them."

11

"Do that. Drop flares. The boy at the bridge have any idea how far behind that mountain it was when he saw it fall?"

"Naw, he's a stupid grunt." Waldo said into his hand phone, "Yonkers three-one, three-one, this two-four, flare mission, over."

Waldo's battalion Fire Direction Control Center was in the middle of the battalion area in basecamp, the camp's best-fortified above-ground bunker. Concrete foundations and a concrete slab floor supported six-by-six uprights keeping four layers of plastic-woven sandbags in neat military order for a roof. The inner walls were reinforced with perforated steel planking, the same used to cover the Golf Course — the basecamp airstrip — and that hung with plywood for the huge plastic-sheathed maps that covered the walls. The portholes were heavily shuttered and the overhead cover three feet thick. In that immense heap of organized sand was a small, dark hole filled almost completely with a plotting table of plywood on sawhorses made from wood scrounged from ammo crates. Bare bulbs overhead. Radios against the wall. The computers worked with pencil and rule at their plotting boards in a suffocating, dank, dusty, dark atmosphere, sand dripping from the ceiling when enemy mortar rounds ranged over the bunker, old burger wrappers from the Airborne Club strewn on the rickety metal chairs.

The radio telephone operator on duty relayed Waldo's commands to the basecamp guns, six dirty brown 105mm howitzers with the power to burst eardrums with their roar, the gunbunnies opening the breeches between their trails for the projos to be rammed home. *WHAM WHAM WHAM!* and the fifty pound rounds of steel and power were sizzling overhead beyond the two green mountains and there, *there!* in the black and gray fog the flares burst, one after the other, in neat timed order so that there was always light, the flares sinking through the clouds on their parachutes flaming pink like angels descending into the wrong world. "Good," Waldo said into the mike, "good," and he tramped forward through the brush following Fruitcake, speaking softly into his hand phone adjusting the flares.

Captain Foley heard the whispered words, "Mikes comin' through," and got off the trail with Bravo, blinking his magnified eyes behind his thick lenses, his brows bobbing up and down. He dropped the utility strap from his shoulder and let his '16 rest there across his hip, aimed at the trail, the safety off and his finger on the trigger. The point man for the Viet militia company, the Mikes, came through the brush grinning to hide the fright in his eyes, his bush hat wrapped with his blue Mike scarf and his own fresh bright new M-16 in his hands. He waved at Foley and trudged uptrail following the route Fruitcake had cut. Fruitcake was up there, having heard the whispers even where he was, crouching by the side of the trail with his rifle on go-go, waiting. The lead element came up, the Mike captain hissing commands at men too miserable in the cold rain to hear, fright in their eyes, too: What were they doing out after dark, risking their lives for a Yank chopper down? To hell with the Yankees and their filthy war. Don't they know the dead crawl around up here at night? The Mike company went up the trail into the dark giggling, passing cigs, waving their flashlights around.

The Bravos closed up trail behind them, cursing. "Fruitcake," said Foley, "follow those bastards so long as they're heading south into the valley. If they don't, you cut trail and keep us away from them."

"Yeah, Daddy." Fruitcake loped off into the fog swirling behind the Mikes, the last Mike with huge startled eyes gazing back at him.

Next came the company lead – the captain, his radioman and one gunman, the company's best killer, B-2. B-2 was range-scrawny and with a Hollywood vanity that forced him to shave even in the jungle. He had pale, wet, nervous eyes in sacks of black bagging heavily on his cheeks. He had come to the Bravos from the mechanized infantry where he'd survived a rocket through the side of his track — he was sitting on top, of course, and he was blown off and walked away from the wreck laughing to have been forgotten by death, this time. He walked away from the mech, too, because that rocket had used up all his luck in one *whoof!* of murder. A man can take one B-40 plastique shaped charge through his track and laugh out of his chattering teeth, but he won't go back to the

13

boxes and try it again, not if he's sane. B-2 considered himself too sane to die.

Sergeant Mars was part of the company lead but now he was back with the tail of the column, watching for Chucks creeping up on them. Where the Mikes went, Chuck was sure to follow. Sergeant Mars slogged along, watching behind for Chuck and listening ahead for the dying chopper.

The Bee was sergeant of the First Platoon and took his plat's lead behind the company lead. Even after six months in Vietnam his face still bubbled with water blisters. He ran a hand over them and burst them. The feel of the fog was good on the wounds. The Bee was not a risk-taking man but he did believe in taking advantage of the ridiculous enthusiasms of others. Which is why he liked marching behind the captain. He followed exactly in Daddy's big footprints, placing his foot in each soppy mark made in the mud by the captain. No .30 bullet planted under the trail on top of a nail was going to blow a hole through *his* foot. If anyone was going to trip a mine or a jump-up grenade, let it be Daddy. That would give The Bee time to jump howling away or maybe hit the deck.

The rain did not slacken. Ahead, in the saddle of the two mountains, the angel flares came down. The ground underfoot oozed slime and smelled of rot. The trees around them were leafless. The helis had defoliated this area. They crossed three tiny streams. Water sloshed in their jungle boots and ran out the drain holes. It was cold, their teeth chattered. The air smelled like old socks.

For a moment The Bee shut out the sounds of the men around him and listened only to the jungle — water dripping, weed hissing in the night breeze, small animals frightened from their holes by the tramping feet, somewhere under the lid of night a brushbuck barked. You shouldn't be out in the rain, little brother, thought The Bee.

It was as though he was the first man ever to set foot here on this slope, the ground so new and rich he could almost believe his fantasy. He thought: If I stop for a moment here in the black rain around this bend of trail, I'll be alone. He thought: Do it now! Step left off the trail and be alone. Be free. Disappear. *Go home!* He thought: Vietnam is a place a man can live the whole of his life under skies as intense as cymbals' crashing, with dirt roads hot through the soles of your boots, palms and pines of green-yellow and silver, birches by the road, red jungle birds cawing through the sky over stream-cut mountains, air that smells and tastes fresh, a land filled with races of tigers and men and women frightening and exciting.

It was a place where everyone he knew died. Where some few he didn't know crawled home alive. What did it mean to be a soldier in that place? This is what it meant: No one was kind to him. There was no woman to give him a soft word, the women there gave him Cokes filled with battery acid or ground glass or they raised little naked children who held pin-pulled grenades behind their backs. He was hated at home as well. For the first time in his life he was hated by people who didn't know him. That thought struck him with a cold and bitter surprise.

He could not imagine that young man he had once thought himself to be, a young man of crew-cuts and roaring cars, laughing girls burnt in the Colorado sun, reckless pranks, and strange untested ideas about good and evil. He had never suspected those ideas would count for anything. Now he wished he had never heard of the war, that he might have gone his whole life without testing those ideas. The boy who had been himself lived a safer, cleaner, saner life, a more thoughtless life, a life without test and strain. That boy was not the man who was here now slogging this jungle trail dragging his pack and rifle a thousand meters south into the Valley — and tomorrow it would be a thousand meters west toward Pleiku or a thousand meters east toward the South China Sea. But he had the chance to quit right here. Step off the trail and the war was finished.

At the bend he stepped offtrail and pushed into the brush. He squatted there watching the company pass, laughing to himself at how easily he had escaped the war. His body shook with his silent laughter and the chill rain. It was over. All over. He had been poor and ragged and ashamed and suddenly it was over! He had stepped out of life. He put the muzzle of his '16 into his mouth, put his finger on the wet trigger, and pressed. The firing pin *thunked* into the round and nothing happened. "My '16

15

doesn't misfire!" he wanted to shout. "Not *my* '16!" But it had. It was a sign: He was not going to die in Vietnam. He was surprised to learn the news and have this perfect proof of it. The certainty put him beyond the power of strangers' hate, and he could do his soldier's job.

He ejected the bad round, broke it apart to deny it to Chuck, chambered another, and climbed out of the brush onto the trail where Sergeant Mars, the last man in the column, stood staring at him. Mars grabbed him by the collar and shoved him uptrail with a kick in the rump and on they went in their endless plodding shambling into the Valley.

* * *

From Mars at the tail of the column to Fruitcake on the point lost in the fog and elephant grass ahead, every man in the column was drifting through his own private reverie. It was a column of ghost soldiers marching through the enemy's dangerous country, dreaming that the war would end. They had forgotten their mission — the helicopter — in their hard slogging through the mud and rain, climbing the mountainside, the stink of Viet cigarettes coming back to them from the Mikes ahead, and the Mikes, terrified in the dark, flashing their lights around the mountainside to warn off Chuck or to frighten him away or to make the Yanks targets of Chuck's mortars, all that irritating the G.I.s. But nothing irritated them enough to break them free of their dreams, the dreams that saved them from the bleeding pack sores on their shoulders and rumps and the wet coldness in their stumbling wood feet. There were no bennies tonight to ease the pain. No one ate bennies in Chuck's night. The bourbon in Mars's canteen was untasted. There is no point in a soldier's thinking on his mission once he has decided to see it through. They went on.

Mars had spent this day in the war as he had spent so many days — all of the days — of his four years there, living without thinking about living, living with all thoughts covered because some part of his mind was traitor to the other part. In war a soldier cannot think beyond the moment or he will die. Back in Burgerland, his wife and kids can be sprawled on the beach slurping ice cream cones and so pass a long, lazy day thinking they've done well to spend their time so easily. But their soldier father-husband half a world away has lived a dozen lifetimes in their one beach day: A soldier gains or loses one life each time he grovels in the mud, hiding shrieking from enemy steel. Some soldiers, such as the gunman B-2, win lives now and then, and carefully husband what they've won. Others, and Mars was always one of the others, lose one life in each fight. How many lives had he to left to lose? Mars would know only when the last life was yanked away from him and he stood there naked to the enemy. Mars had no *family*, though he had a wife and three children he had not seen twice in four years. The army offered him home leaves and sometimes he took them at home and sometimes in Australian whorehouses. Was it the war or fear of his wife that made him stay four years in Vietnam when rational men were happy to go home whole after one year? He preferred to think it was the war.

It was a morbid night and his mind crowded with morbid thoughts of the future. Some nights here smelled of clover and others of walnuts. He loved the days especially when the air was pale, light, and unburdened. Evenings, clouds would pillow on Hong Kong Mountain, sinking over basecamp, and the tough grass would crinkle under his boots as he walked through the camp with its tang of diesel and urine from the johns. The camp was filled with five thousand soldiers only five hundred of whom ever left the camp for combat, the rest passed their days counting bubblegum at the Post Exchange.

* * *

Mars was not a born soldier. Few men are. He was made a soldier. After an unremarkable but cold six months in the Korean conflict, in which he drew first blood on the enemy he always seemed to be fighting, and after eight years in a Stateside army post peeling spuds and wishing he were somewhere else, after a boost to corporal – and those were the grand old days when there were corporals in the army, now the wartime

17

army was full of "Specialists" this class and that, but Specialists in what?
— he had the two gold chevrons sewn on his sleeves and was proud of
them. He was made an acting sergeant, too, and that could have been
made permanent with some hard work and good reports. But he did a
soldierly thing and took an Irish buck sergeant into the coal room and beat
him silly for the sake of a woman. The buck pulled a bayonet he had
planted in the coal and Mars barely had the presence of mind to kick the
buck in the head, ending the fight without bloodshed. The sergeant wob-
bled a bit when Mars put him on his feet and booted him homeward, but
he was okay. The bayonet went into the furnace.

It wasn't the fight that cost him his two new stripes, it was the bayonet
in the furnace. He'd wasted U.S. Government Property. The Irish top
sergeant was decent about it. No Article 15 before the captain, just no
stripes, and out of the company into the Rathole, the holding company
where the regiment kept its misfits — the homosexuals, the degenerates,
the Georgia clowns who figured they could get out of their draft time by
beating up junior officers. They were all waiting out their processing time
to collect their Dishonorables and that bus ticket home. He hated the
Rathole. He was a soldier and proud of it, though he had been nothing but
a potato-peeling career private up to then. There was one way out of the
holding company and that was Vietnam. After Korea, war didn't frighten
him. He volunteered. The army was glad to have him in the quota, it
meant one fewer draftee to drag out of the rioting and rebellious popula-
tion of the Burgerland young.

Everything about Vietnam was strange to him and nothing was anything like what they'd told him to expect. They'd dropped him on the
South China Sea coast and he'd tramped around a sort of jungly desert
that later was called the Street Without Joy, but the 50th Mech, the 69th
Armored, and the 17th Artillery knew it as the Bong Son Plain, a place
where every tree harbored a Chuck. They were good smart Chucks, who
set traps for tanks and blew them away, who set traps for grunts and blew
them away, who set traps for the guns and blew them away. There was
nothing to save the Yanks but the Hawkeyes, a half dozen pilots in little

Birddog aircraft flimsy as kites who would go up and get crazy at all the Chucks they'd see. When they'd call down the ambushes they'd sighted, the Batcos – the battalion commanders – would ignore them and send in the tanks and the grunts World War II-style. But they weren't fighting the Nazis or the Japanese. They were fighting Chuckie in another dimension of warfare and they couldn't get at him. But he could get at them. It was unfair that the U.S. Army was that stupid.

What saved Private Mars was the battleship *New Jersey*. She skulked off the coast and when the Hawkeyes or the ground artillery spotters called in her fire, Mars thought, Who needs nukes or the Air Force if ya got the *Jersey*? He had thought eight-inch howitzers punching out their hundred-and-fifty-pound shells could tear up a piece of real estate, but when that lady off the coast turned her guns on Vietnam, there was no Vietnam left. She loved to run range and deflection spreads or rolling fires that plowed up and plowed up and plowed up the land, flashing all over orange and black, chunks of steel the size of Volkswagens *zinging* crashing overhead. Old Chuckie didn't like that lady – she came after him from another world and it was a world he couldn't touch.

The 69th Armored was a skull-taking outfit. They paraded into battle with Chuck heads bleeding on their tanks. That magic did them no good – on the Plain, they were torn to pieces. Mars was among them when it happened. His second week in the war and nothing was as it was supposed to be, nothing but the lady. He rode into battle with his shining bald head camouflaged under a bush hat and with two weeks' Nam experience. Already he had had his second Combat Infantryman's Badge for his dress greens, proving that he had stepped before the fire in two wars and had lived. He didn't want any of the other badges, the Purple Puke or the B.S., because he had already seen what a man had to pay to get them. In they went holding the rear of the tank turrets and standing over the grates pumping hot air from the tank engines, the mech infantry tracks streaming alongside with all their G.I.s sitting on top of the boxes. He was with a

Navy corpsman from the *Jersey*, some fool who thought he could get himself a C.I.B. and volunteered to hump the radio for the artillery Forward Observer who was there with Mars, too.

It was a good fight. It lasted thirty seconds. Chuck was happy with the results. A platoon each of mech and armor was wiped out. It was fog or smoke from the *Jersey*'s fire that clouded the field and saved Mars's life. He lolled back along his poncho, pulled it over his bleeding bald head and turned his face against the ground. Babies cried. Phantoms slithered past. Purple mists shifted densely around his face. Odors of sweat and rotting alien things trembled in the fog. He began to sob over his shattered M-16. Silence! His ears twisted and sucked. Were they coming back? Was he the only one left alive? Emptiness! His body began to stiffen at the joints and he thought he was dying. Better to die now in this quiet peace than let Chuckie take him with his knives. He turned slowly, curling into a comma, the muscles of his throat pulling his lips from his teeth. He could feel himself take on the appearance of a dead man. He was dying. Thank God!

He couldn't feel his hands or feet. He ground his face into the earth, whimpering. Along his side only the oozing wound was animate. He made himself a lump of ground, waiting for the half moon of night to brush his camouflage poncho and hide him. With evening or dawning, he didn't know which, he began to disappear. Tigers passed him and fed on the corpses of others. Cobras holding their hoods waist-high slicked over his plastic sheet trailing sweet-smelling slime. A single water buffalo dunged on the stubs of his legs. Only his tears remained material. Where were the choppers? Why hadn't the army cleared this field? He rolled open one eye and watched as masses of fog cartwheeled around the clearing, carving back the jungle, leaving nothing but Chuck faces staring at him from the trees, phantoms that came toward him. He screamed but his tongue had disappeared. Their tentacles plucked away his uniform. Their flesh was cold and rough. The tallest nudged him over on his back, grunted, and turned to walk away.

Mars's body came alive: "Help me! Help me!" he cried.

The fog burst apart, blue sky rushed into the clearing.

"Not catatonic after all," said the tallest G.I. "You can get up now, buddy."

"No, he can't. Look at that hole in his side."

"Kee-rist, what a mess! Thought him a shirker or a coward. Help him up, you two."

The tall one, the N.C.O., detailed two men to drag Mars along. There was no time for a medevac chopper and the field was still hot, so they had to run for it. The fight had lasted thirty seconds and Mars had been there in his delirium five minutes more before they had found him.

He staggered toward the jungle between his rescuers and found the Navy corpsman's brainless head, eyes sunk back, the great pink cavity lined with veins. He dipped his fist into its emptiness, searching for whatever silver threads there are that make men men. In that moment he believed he saw that there is no mystery to life: We are all animals and no one survives.

2.

On the Bravos staggered, uphill, some of them thinking dimly about the downed helicopter, wondering if they would find survivors. Had the chopper fried them? Had Chuck vivisected them? It was all the same to the worried-eyed cowboy B-2, slogging along there behind Captain Daddy, a post he had assumed for himself because the captain was such a clumsy oaf everyone knew he'd let himself be blown away if B-2 weren't there to bodyguard him. B-2 was part of a different war. His war had all the dreariness and confusion of all the other wars being fought that night on the mountainside, but his war was a war with Purpose: Vietnam was going to make him rich.

To the forty-one others in Bravo Company, plus Waldo the artilleryman who was not a grunt but attached to them from the redleg battalion, B-2 was an old-fashioned berserker, something belonging on a Viking ship or with Duke William howling up Hastings Hill to cross sword and ax with King Harold. General Custer could have used him. He stood in his fights yelling and spraying bullets at the enemy — for him the enemy seemed hill, tree, stone, as much as men — and putting his body between his buddies and death. B-2 knew he should not be alive, he had taken too many stupid chances. But he expected to survive this war, unlike those who accepted the terrifying statistics: Only on in twelve U.S. soldiers actually fought. Of the infantry, each combat soldier would be wounded once, each officer twice, too often that meant dead. B-2 would survive because he had Purpose. It had been a long dirty day months ago that had led to the moment that gave him Purpose.

* * *

B-2 had been in the mechanized infantry then.

Dirty Dave, a lieutenant who was a dandy in the dirt — tall, clean-skinned, a pencil mustache and a stupid red beret – "Let him wear that idiot thing," his plat would say, "and attract steel away from *us*" — led them through bright, boring days crashing through the boonies, knocking down trees with their tracks, plinking at tin cans with their stolen .45s, chopping off branches with machinegun fire, getting the boxes' tracks stuck in the mud. Armored personnel carriers bog down easily when they fight in the wrong terrain in the wrong war. They throw track bumping into trees. With two platoons — eight boxes — and their commanding officer along for the ride and Dirty Dave's box in the lead, they had to stop for four mechanical failures and seven stickings in thigh-deep mud. They spent six hours in the hill country, traveling four miles on the tops of those hot, hard boxes, muscles bruised and stiff, skin peeling, those foolish too-heavy-to-wear helmets on their heads – they wore them that day to satisfy their commanding officer – the C.O. – who hated them, too, but had to please the battalion commander who never left his battalion area in base-camp, his beer, and his burgers, but who totted up the written reports of the numbers of his troops who wore their helmets. Branches slapped their faces. Fat black and yellow spiders dropped from the bamboo and scamp-ered over them. The water simmered in their canteens. Sun baked. The world stank of dust, grease, sweat and diesel smoke. More breakdowns, more mud, more of every rotten thing. After a full morning of that non-sense the mech infantry forgot about looking for Chucks and started looking for an easy route home, tracing it on the artilleryman's map. They found a boobytrap and some old foxholes and blew them, some diversion.

But no enemy. All through this ordinary day the C.O. cracked dull jokes and diddled his own bushier mustache and stood in the thickest mud working on the stuck tracks. He was happy, he was imperturbable, he irritated everyone. They didn't realize this outing away from the Batco – the battalion commander – was a lark for their commander, like a boy let out of school by surprise.

Vietnam was a war of military intelligence, or so the senior officers believed. They believed that good intel was more important than good soldiering. That a day studying maps and photos in basecamp was a day closer to rotation home and a safer day than prowling the woods with the grunts. If the soldiering couldn't achieve the results the intel promised, the reports to higher simply needed a little more creative writing than usual. Every level had its intel and every level had its reports. A field body count of two Killed in Action and two Wounded in Action V.C.-suspect became, when at battalion level, six K.I.A. and twenty W.I.A. confirmed V.C./N.V.A. Batt justified it simply: You could never count on those stupid grunts to have the guts to actually go poking through those booby-trapped woods to collect all the meat after a firefight, so some additional number had to be added for accuracy's sake — and if arty was used that meant some bods just got atomized or blown up into treetops and another percentage had to be counted in. As the report climbed the ladder to brigade, to division, to corps, to the commanding general's desk, it grew from that original two and two to twenty killed and a hundred wounded V.C./N.V.A./Laotians. What most struck the G.I.s in the field as odd about the system was that the general actually seemed to believe the reports he was fed, even though he had done the same type of screwy reporting himself in the last war he'd fought. While the intel reports going up the chain were inflated and believed, intel coming down the chain was reported scrupulously and just as scrupulously disbelieved by the G.I.s in the field.

* * *

The morning of the day B-2 found Purpose, official word had trickled down to their company commander that higher headquarters expected a general uprising throughout Two Corps Tactical Zone beginning at exactly 0900, higher always believing in Chuck's adherence to precision in his plans. The company commander ignored the warning. Just at the moment their first track bogged down in mud in Chuckie's wild woods, the enemy hit Landing Zone Action with its firebase of six howitzers and hit Pump Station Number 3 on this side of the Mang Yang Pass, using mortars and recoilless rifles. The company commander followed the action around their Area of Operations on his blue net radio. It was like watching T.V. — a lot of fun and no pain for him. He stood in the mud with his shovel digging out the stuck track and whistled some old rock-and-roll song no one else could identify.

Then the Hawkeyes in their little spotter planes reported two platoons of Viet Cong and later a company of eighty men in blue and gray North Vietnamese Army uniforms with .30 machineguns and Russian 82mm mortars. That was serious news. For a moment. The commander stood in the mud with his shovel in his hands and waited for the next report: Ah, yes – the enemy had slyly intermingled with civilian woodcutters and the artillery couldn't shoot them in there among ordinary folk. The enemy vanished. As always. Provided what was seen was seen. He went back to his mud-digging and his unidentifiable song.

The radio reported that a Mike Force, the Vietnamese highly irregular militia, skirmished in the southwest with the V.C. A Ruffpuff home guard day ambush made a minor contact and then overran a V.C.-prone village and pulled some AK-47 automatic rifles and rocket-propelled grenades from the village well. That marked the high point of the general uprising and an ordinary day in the highlands where the five armies staring eyeball to eyeball had no interest in fighting so long as things stayed as they were. After all, the war was about to end. Everybody everywhere knew it. Why stir things up and maybe get dead? What made the day unusual was the money.

Dirty Dave was bored and whining and too dainty to get himself muddy around while the commander and his troops once again shoveled aside heaps of fetid jungle earth to pry the command and control track out of the mud, so the commander sent him out to recon the surrounding hills. Dave adjusted his red beret and dabbed a little theatrical mud on the shine of his cheeks and led out happily before his plat had time to form up. They straggled after him.

Away from the mud, the flies, the sweat, the army was a lark again, and they were hunting. They humped an hour into the hills before the pleasure of their freedom began to wear and their minds turned to thoughts of chow and cool water. B-2 spotted him — one Chuck running like hell through the brush — and saved them all from boredom. The tree cover wasn't thick enough to worry a mortar round. Dirty Dave walked fire from the 60mm mortar — a tube the size of the cardboard center of a roll of kitchen towels — and dropped steel on the Chuck, howling, "Busted his ass, right on, hey!" and then scrambled after him, the others following more cautiously, to see what the dead Chuck had in his pack to split up for the spoils of war.

The blood trail stopped in the grass. As though the Chuck had jumped up into the sky and disappeared. "Spider hole, gotta be a spider hole 'round here," said Dave, drawing his bayonet and digging into the earth for the hidden entrance. "Get some frags ready. B-2, stand by to blast him if he pops up in my face."

"We really shouldn't do this, Lieutenant," said B-2, the great bruised sacks of worry in which his eyes sat heavier and grayer. "Where's the one Chuck, there's more."

The platoon streamed from the woods and bunched around the spider hole. B-2 said to them, "They likely got covering M.G.s in other holes – fan out, you guys."

"Naw, this guy was just an observer for 'em," said Dirty Dave. "There!" He slid his bayonet under the lip of the hole's lid and swung up the false covering of sod and matting on a tunnel gleaming with blood. No one to be seen in it. "Flashlight," he called. He started to climb in.

27

"Could be booby-trapped, Lieutenant," said B-2.

"Frag it then."

Dave stood back. They threw in grenades. He dropped the matted lid in place and it popped up with the grenade blasts, Dave marveling at the frisbee spin of the thing. Dave climbed into the blood-slimy hole, motioning B-2 to follow. "Can't be too deep for only one guy. Where's the R.T.O.? Bring the radio just in case."

The radioman protested: "Radio won't do you much good down there, Lieutenant."

"Come on, come on!"

The R.T.O. followed and saved his own life. As he went into the hole, the last of the platoon streamed out of the trees and stood gawking into the pit. The enemy's covering machineguns opened fire. The three of them — B-2, Dirty Dave, and the R.T.O. — tumbled deep into the pit, smearing themselves with the Chuck's blood, and found themselves at the conjunction of three tunnels weakly lit by candles.

"Good God," whispered the radioman, "this ain't no spider hole. This's a regimental command post!"

They gawked at each other as the machinegun firing racketed overhead, and the screams.

"What do we do now?" said B-2.

Dirty Dave pulled tight his red beret and said, "Follow the blood trail and hope we find an exit through another spider hole and jump out and flank 'em or run like hell."

They went crouching through the narrow tunnels following the blood and found the corpse heaped on a platform carved from the earth — a bed, perhaps — in a tunnel that was slightly larger and equipped like a squad bay with bedrolls, rucksacks, cooking stoves vented through shafts to the forest floor above. The place was empty and mothballed, waiting for action. They found the strongbox. A U.S. Army footlocker painted with Chuck symbols. Tally sheets were strewn in the dirt. The lock was open. Here must be souvenirs – a brass N.V.A. belt buckle with the star on it or some Chuck flags or Chicom pistols. B-2 flung open the trunk. The thing was full of money. Bright crisp Burgerland dollars. The Fu Manchu stuff the Arvins used. Strange Commie currency. "Must be a million or more!" said Dave, grabbing up packs of hundreds.

"Got to be counterfeit," said B-2. "Forget it. Let's go."

"No, no, no," said the R.T.O. "This here is a Chuck paymaster station and this is *real*. They don't pay their boys counterfeit."

They stuffed their pockets and packs.

"We tell the others," said Dave, "but this can't get back to batt."

"Whadya mean? This is spoils of war. They can't take it from us," said B-2.

"U.S. Army don't take spoils," said the R.T.O. "That's in the regs."

"We keep our mouths shut," said Dave. He led out, greed filling him with a new and unaccustomed energy. He and B-2 went up the last tunnel together, the R.T.O. hanging back and showing good sense, firing their '16s go-go and sweeping the tunnel clean, clambering over four bods and a wrecked M.G. and throwing off a spider hole lid shouting to the others in the platoon as Dave and B-2 opened defilade fire on the enemy machineguns. They had been in the tunnels sixty seconds and had almost missed the fight. Now the reformed platoon poured fire and grenades onto the enemy and the R.T.O. called in a gunship strike. They rolled all their teargas grenades down the holes, yipping away from the tendrils of eye-watering gas sprouting from unexpected spider holes in strange parts of the forest.

The fight was over in minutes, much less time than it took the C.O. and the rest of the company to slog through the jungle to relieve them. The cost was three U.S. dead and twelve wounded out of Dirty Dave's twenty-man platoon, only Dave, B-2, and the R.T.O. unscathed, though the radioman had enough shakes to make him useless the rest of the day.

The C.O. forgot the casualty toll when Dave had them haul into the sunshine the footlocker full of money. The split was fairly made with only Dave's plat and the C.O. getting double shares. But American soldiers are greedy and even that fair split wasn't good enough for some who yakked their heads off back in basecamp. What had been reported to the

Batco as a sensational fight and victory without mention of the money suddenly became a treasure hunt for the Batco and the Military Police, the Mamas and Papas. The company was quarantined, shaken down, and two million dollars in green and Vietnamese currency recovered, not counting what the M.P.s and the Batco stuffed in their pockets before the count began.

Only a few of the company had had the foresight to hide their spoils of war immediately after returning to base, and those now were afraid to tell the others of their good fortune. Three of them finally made it home alive with their shares, joining the army cooks who had sold army meat on the black market and then served their own men the cheap, infected local beef and pocketed the difference and senior N.C.O.s who went partners in whorehouses that served both Yanks and Chucks as men who had made good profits on the war.

B-2, for some reason sensible only to his greed, believed the army had stolen from him $150,000 in spoils, his calculation of what he had in his fatigue pockets when the Batco brought in the M.P.s. That was his legal share. He meant to have it all back. The army could recompense him by giving him another shot at some spoils or he would do the American thing and sue the army for his money. Either way was fine with him so long as he got his share. Getting his share was his Purpose in the war.

* * *

The trail grew rougher and stormier as Bravo Company climbed the mountainside. The rougher trail gave them better footing. The rain slackened and blew away with the fog and the mountain, old and humpbacked, called Old Baldy, stood in sharp relief against the velvet black sky and its stars. The sudden end of the rain frightened the Mikes up ahead. They opened fire against the mountain.

Cursing, B-2 flung himself down alongside Captain Foley and Waldo. Waldo had his radio handset to his face and was ready to call for artillery fire, but the tracers skittering back over the company were good American orange tracers coming out of M-16 rifles and not enemy green from AK-47s.

"Bee!" shouted the captain. "Tell 'em to stay down and don't shoot unless I say!"

"It's just the damn Mikes, Captain," The Bee shouted. "We won't hurt 'em, promise."

Waldo turned off his radio and lay back on his pack. He was hungry again. His arms and legs were torn and battered by tree limbs, thorns, whipping elephant grass. His mind was tired, his spirit bruised. Forty-two lives depended on him: He was the man with the big guns. He believed there was nothing his artillery could not do. He was Bravo Company's bodyguard with 133 days to go on his tour. But he felt like a man who has used up all strength and luck in mistakes and still must face the dragon.

Captain Daddy, the Missouri parson, squeezed Waldo's arm, saying, "It's okay, boy, it's okay. Ya just gotta cope," and surprised Waldo back into the war.

The ridiculous racketing rifle fire upslope slacked off into yips of pain as the Mikes came tumbling back downtrail wide-eyed and frightened. "Let 'em pass, let 'em pass!" shouted the captain. "Good riddance." The G.I.s shouted insults, tripping the Mikes with their rifles. Down by the rear guard where Sar'n Mars held power the G.I.s slammed the arrogant Mike captain against a tree and beat him for a coward. The captain was pleased with his blood and bruises, they would support his lies to his own higher about his great firefight with Chuck while the G.I.s cowered in the rain.

With the Mikes gone and nothing ahead but the star-glittering night and the mountain, Captain Foley led out, whispering for Fruitcake to fall back to report. After all that noise, they'd have to cut new trail now to avoid Chuck zeroing in on them with mortars. Fruitcake made no response. They found him shot through the head by a Mike M-16. The round had done the explosive damage that only a mean little '16 can do. Half his brain sprawled in the mud.

Waldo, Daddy, B-2, and The Bee stood over the wreckage of the country boy. Nothing was said. What could be said? His luck had run out, as it would for each of them if they stayed in this war long enough. A cold and tearless send-off, maybe, but soldiers can waste no tears in the field.

"What'll we do with him?" asked Waldo. Great God, he thought, I've failed again – one after the other, I lose them.

"We'll have to leave him here," said the captain, thinking, One more, one more, must all of them die in this place?

"We can't call dustoff in this storm," said The Bee, "and we can't detail anyone to carry him back down."

Foley ran two gloved fingers over his eyes magnified behind his thick lenses held onto his face by the little strap and cleared his eyes. "No, we can't do anything for him," he said.

B-2 bent over the corpse. "You'll have to take his things, Daddy, so's those stinking Mikes don't come back and rob the bod. We don't want Chuck to get his weapon, ammo nor boots." It's all accident, mistake, and luck, isn't it? B-2 marveled. There's no skill in war. You're cannon fodder or you're not, you're dead or not. You find a million bucks or you don't.

The Bee took Fruitcake's M-16 and handed it to Waldo. "Souvenir of Vietnam," he said, and he began to cry. He squatted by the blown-up head and touched Fruitcake. That was all the ceremony Fruitcake had. There would be time and peace enough for more back in Burgerland, after the body had been recovered, washed, salted and iced, and stuffed in its black plastic bag, cased twice in metal, and airmailed to Mama.

Foley took off his bush hat: "You were a good boy," he said to the body. He put the hat on backwards. B-2 fixed it for him. Foley tried to rub his eyes again and punched his fingers into his eyeglasses.

B-2 pulled off one of Fruitcake's dog tags and handed it to the captain: "I'd better cut trail now, Daddy," he said, trudging into the elephant grass.

Peepsite came forward to take over B-2's bodyguarding of the captain. He turned his lopsided face from the corpse and said, "I never want to be here again."

The Bee knew he had no reason to squat beside the body bawling silently — he considered himself a suicide on his second life — but it all came out of him, everything he could not name, and he wept over the dead boy.

Foley clapped him on the shoulder and said, "Shake it off, Bee, ya gotta be alert out here. Get going up front."

The Bee left Foley and Waldo to arrange the body in a respectable way and to lead on the company. Each man came past Fruitcake's ruin in somber thankfulness that it was Fruitcake and not him. Each determined to shoot a stupid Mike first chance he got.

* * *

Waldo pulled himself to his feet from the trail mud and watched the leading elements of Bravo plunge upslope behind The Bee, marching toward the downed chopper. I'm responsible for them and I fail them, he said, silently, to the night. Will they all die because of me? Trembling with cold and fear of failure, he settled the pack frame on his back and trudged uptrail. He was the redleg, the artilleryman, and his redemption depended upon bringing them back alive.

Redemption for murder. The people of a nation tell their soldiers that war is not murder but justifiable homicide. Fifth Commandment happily suspended. But the first killing is always murder. None of the killing that comes after means as much. None of the killing that comes after is as difficult. Waldo's sin was failure of himself but his crime was murder. The longer his war lasted, the greater the chance to cleanse his darkened soul.

It was the seventeenth day in Waldo's war. His first combat mission. His new army mustached tickled. After this day, he shaved it off. He was filled with fear that he would fail this mission, he would show himself incompetent to be a soldier. But the cool professionalism of the Hawkeye pilot relieved him. The pilot had eight months in the war on this tour and three spotter planes shot out from under him. He was an old-timer who

33

knew what he was doing, steeled in the horrors of the Bong Son Plain, where centuries earlier Private Mars had learned his lessons about this kind of war. Waldo wanted desperately to make a good show for this old-timer, to prove himself as man and soldier.

"That's the Song Ba we passed over?" Waldo asked into the intercom, peering down from the backseat of the little plane at the river as slick and black as obsidian pouring between scruffy brown hills.

"Rog. What's our logger now?" said the pilot.

"We're, uh, location off the map!" Waldo frantically stretched the map in hopes of finding some part of it that showed him where they were. "We're off the map and out of my arty range!" he cried. He pushed his nose flat on the plexiglass window, hoping to see something – a mountain, a road – to tell him where they were up here in all this air.

He peered down at the riverbank where hundreds of fishing poles were jammed in the soft earth. "Are those enemy fishing poles?"

"Yep," said the pilot, twisting the Birddog around and up to seven hundred feet. Waldo's stomach twisted around and up with it.

Waldo began to sweat in the cold of the little cabin, wind whistling through cracks in the thin, worn fuselage. Where are we? What am I supposed to do? He stared stupidly at the back of the pilot's flight helmet. He looked down at the fishing poles. He said, "This is still easy rifle range!"

"Don't sweat it. I've lost three 'dogs and I'm still up here." The pilot lit a cigarette.

Waldo sank back into his seat, his flak vest chafing his chin and wet armpits, his stomach full of vomit, his lungs gasping for air, the heavy flight helmet causing his head to ache. The sweat matting his shirt to his chest and back turned cold.

"Hey!" cried the pilot from the intercom. The plane spun over and dived at the black river. Waldo groaned as the bile rose in his throat. "There's a guy swimming in the river!" Waldo flattened his nose against the window and gaped down at the water. The windows shrieked, the engine clashed, the pilot swung the plane swooshing down in a huge tubercular clatter, the fuselage skin rippling, Waldo grinding his teeth, gripping his turning stomach. "See him by the log?" shouted the pilot.

"Where?"

"Get a smoke!"

Waldo lunged at the grenade rack, his fingers pulling every wrong strap, sweat stinging his eyes. A smoke grenade fell into his lap. He yanked the ring, shoved the grenade through the narrow side window, and held it at arm's length.

"Drop it!" shouted the pilot. "Drop it, drop!"

Waldo flung the grenade at the river. It burst early. A purple cloud gushed up toward the plane. The plane bent and leaped around the smoke like a cat chasing a mouse, orbiting back on the man swimming in the river.

"I don't see the smoke anymore!" cried Waldo.

"You threw it in the water, you idiot! I see him — he's swimming for shore!" The pilot jammed the plane forward. Waldo slapped against the belts holding him in his canvas seat. "Forget the redleg, Waldo. This guy's mine. I'm gonna let him have it with the rockets!"

"But he's just down there swimming, for Christ's sake!" Waldo cried. And then he was stunned at what he had said. But he said: "You can't kill a man for that! For just swimming!"

The startled pilot yanked the plane away from the attack, the cigarette jutting up, smoke puffing from his nostrils clouding the windscreen. He twisted around angrily in his seat. "What's the matter with you? He's not supposed to be down there, right? This is a free-fire zone, right? So he's not a friendly, right? So we kill him, right?" The pilot swung back to his controls. "All right, God damn it, Waldo, this is a redleg mission this flight – I'm just the driver – the decision's yours – *you* tell me what we do."

Seventeen days into the war. Waldo full of untested American decency. He had not yet killed a man. Here was the moment peering up at him from a black river. From the face of a man swimming away a lazy afternoon out of his own war. Doing the thing Waldo suddenly wished he were doing instead of being up here doing what he was doing.

"It's all up to you," said the pilot. "Tell me what you want."

"Up to me?" cried Waldo.

"Yeah, up to you."

Waldo trembled, he shivered. He thrust his arms across his chest to stop the spasm and to grab some warmth. How could it be so cold at just seven hundred feet? Sweat streamed over his face. He was caught in the trap he had made for himself. He saw that. It was the trap that he had made waiting for himself when he enlisted in the army, when he volunteered for the war, when he came out here with his big guns and when he promised himself he would prove himself a man by facing down the demon death and maybe, just maybe, go home a hero, at least to himself. But where is the justice, he wanted to shout, in killing a man whose sole offense is to be caught swimming and helpless on the very day I happen to be hunting men to kill? In that moment he learned that no man should be killed in cold blood. That to go to war for any reason but desperation and there to kill is to commit murder. He was not clever enough or decent enough or brave enough to have thought of that before he came to war. Now he had a bond to be a fighting man. He had signed the contract in oath and now he would sign it in blood. He had to kill, even this kind of killing. He said into the intercom, so quietly he was not sure he had said it at all, "You're right," and his soul began to shrivel.

"We got him!" yelled the pilot, the plane flopping over and lining up on the river, the engine clattering, wings shrieking. Black water, brown earth, heat-shimmering trees spun across the windscreen. The clatter and wail of the dive subsided as the plane lined up on the river. The pilot leaned into the windscreen. It was as though the plane was without an engine swooping into the obsidian stream to smash itself apart – all quiet, all still, no sensation, no movement, nothing. Waldo sat rigid as the plane dived down a five hundred foot cliff of air, like a roller coaster racing downhill at its victim, weirdly stable, strangely heavy, fixed on murder.

Waldo jumped around in his canvas seat to see the four white phosphorous rockets hung under the wing. A lather of white flame! One rocket whipped off from the wing. He faced the river, looking over the pilot's shoulder through the windscreen as the pilot yanked back on the stick, the plane screamed up and around, and Waldo now saw nothing but sky and the cigarette smoke curling out of the pilot's nostrils. He twisted in his seat and peered down at the water and suddenly his ears were filled with the sound of the rocket — *SSSHEEW!* — and the water and phosphorous rose up in a cascading silent blast flecked with magenta, chartreuse, and glittering silver.

His stomach was spinning, his mind circling, the plane in roller-coaster orbit, the water falling back, the pilot leaning against the windscreen staring again at the black river and their target as the plane roared downhill again, again heavy and stable and soundless, swooping for the kill.

"You see him, kid?"

"I don't see a thing," said Waldo, gaping at the white phosphorous fire splashing back into the river, spraying down on leaves and burning holes with its unquenchable chemical flame.

"There he is — I see him!"

The plane rocked over. Vomit rose in Waldo's throat, he trembled and sweated. The second white-smoking rocket jumped from the wing and Waldo twisted around to watch but it was gone. He jerked back to watch it impact in the river and saw it go slow and direct into the body of the enemy swimmer. The plane skidded right and up hard, skimming over the leaping blast of a brilliant *WHOOSH!* of color against the dark water, as though they had smashed stained glass, every bright bit caught in sunlight, tumbling, reflecting all spectrums. Waldo yanked off his flight helmet and threw up into it. He wept.

The pilot over the engine's clattering said from the intercom, "Well, kid, scratch one Chuck. You just got over your first kill and your first two hours of aerial combat time toward your Air Medal. The first one's the hardest. You'll do okay from now on." He lit a second cigarette and passed it back over his shoulder. Waldo took it to drive from his nostrils the smell of his own vomit.

They curved past Hong Kong Mountain standing half in and half out of basecamp, glided over the broad perimeter wire and napalm mines, and settled onto the Golf Course. Waldo jumped from the cold cockpit into a hot afternoon, leaving the soiled flight helmet on the canvas seat. The pilot glanced at it in disgust as Waldo hurried away across the dusty steel-planked airstrip.

Sound came into Waldo's ears and he became aware of the *whip-whip* of three choppers testing engines, of heavy trucks grinding down oiled dirt roads, of jeeps buzzing through grassy fields, of tin shower doors slamming shut echoing across the whole camp, and behind it all lay the *pops!* of the six basecamp howitzers firing a lazy training mission into no man's land. The oiled street was dusty in his nose, his eyes hurt in the too bright sun, his boots grated his ankles.

In the mess hall, he poured coffee to clear the bile from his throat and found another new F.O. in his battered camouflage fatigues, eight days' growth on his face, a combat haircut, an illegal .38 revolver on his hip – his father had sent him that as the army would give him nothing – telling tales of his first combat patrol. But he hadn't yet killed a man. He was entranced with Waldo's better story. They sat in the greasy mess hall, sweat dotting their jackets, the stench of rotted fish paste on the breath of the Viet K.P. girls filling the hall, and Waldo told his better war story. Halfway through the telling, Waldo had heard enough from his own mouth and walked out, his story unfinished, the other F.O. watching him go, startled.

He went into the showers behind his slum barracks, turned on the icy water and got under it, rubbing his fingers over the veins throbbing at his temples, the muscles straining his neck. He pulled off his clothes and boots under the cold water. He stood there until his spirit was numbed.

3.

Bravo slogged onto the crest of Old Baldy, dragging their packs and rifles, exhausted. They had made two thousand meters in five hours, a good day's march but an great accomplishment at night in Chuck's country. They stared down from their perch at the highway far below, the lights winking occasionally from the bunker doors of L.Z. Action there in the hideous maw of Mang Yang Pass and of L.Z. Schueller seven miles east. Farther east were the city limits of basecamp outside the highland village of An Khe, swollen with refugees. A transport plane swung down out of the sky and skimmed to a halt on the Golf Course in front of the lime green control tower built by the French legionnaires. The flyboys preferred night flying, they were afraid of Chuckie's .50 M.G.s that worked by day. A flashlight blazed an instant on Bridge 25, where twenty G.I.s and a couple of tracks hunkered down behind their barbwire barricades and sandbag bunkers to keep the Chucks from blowing the bridge in his night. It was Bridge 25 that had reported seeing the chopper go down in the saddle between Old Baldy and Hill 415.

They turned to face south off the mountain and peered into the lightless murk of the valley where Chuck lived. God, Lucifer, Judas, all those the army is. It is also the good shepherd who, one of its thousands lost, will leave the flock to find the lost sheep. Mother Army peered off that mountain into Chuck's grim night face and though there was fear in them all, there was no doubt in them that they would fulfill their sacred mission.

Captain Foley took the handset from his nervous R.T.O., Kansas City, and called higher on blueleg net: "We're digging in here at our logger for the night. The boys are bushed and I can't risk them in a fight in the open without some rest, over....Roger that. We move out at 0430, out." Foley turned to his one lieutenant and executive officer, First Lieutenant Bad-Henry, an ex-baseball player who might have made pro if the draft had not caught him, a big bluff man with a smile that ran to a rapid twitch if held too long, and fingernails as filthy as a garage mechanic's. "Dig in — slit trenches — we stay here tonight — no cook fires except in the holes, and make sure the boys hunker down with ground cloths over the holes if they cook — we move out in four hours."

Waldo turned away from the wall of black that lay behind Old Baldy. "The gunbunnies won't like to lose the sleep, but I'll have 'em drop a flare in the valley every twenty minutes just so the chopper knows we're still coming for them."

"Do it," said the captain. "Give 'em some hope." He pulled off his glasses and rubbed his eyes swollen from the night march. "I told higher where they could find Fruitcake's body at first light. They'll have the minesweep tank collect it. Sar'n Mars, one man in three sleeps. You and Lieutenant Bad set out the M.G.s and claymore mines. Make it fast — we got four hours' sleep and we're lucky to get that — I want you both rested as well as the men. Waldo, tell me again how many tubes can we call on the Valley?"

"L.Z. Action's got six 105mm howitzers. Schueller's got six more but they can't range more than five miles south of Baldy because they're farther off. They also got two eight-inch howitzers there that can cover us as far as we can walk."

"Good enough," said Foley. "We also got some air cav next door to call for support. If they learned to tell Chuck from us."

With his order of battle set and his night orders given, Captain Foley turned from his two lieutenants — Waldo and Bad-Henry — and his sergeants, faced the valley, and began his prayers as the others drifted off to their duties. It was no Gethsemane of prayer but it was an honest man's prayer — he prayed for deliverance for himself and his boys and then he shut up and let the cosmos have its way. He slept deeply, the only one who slept well that night.

Waldo gouged out his sleeping hole and ate cold muck from cans. Tomorrow night, perhaps, they'd dig in a real Forward Operations Base and he could pop some heat tabs or a bit of plastique and boil up some Lurp rats and eat well, like rice and chicken boiled together with dehydrated peaches. Add to that a taste of stale G.I. powdered coffee and a bite from Mars's bourbon canteen and he would sleep the sleep of a Roman emperor after his feast.

Waldo rolled under his poncho, easing the .45 automatic from its holster, cocking it, flipping on the safety, positioning the pistol on a green handkerchief – to keep it off the dewy earth – on the grass. He put his bush hat over it. He pulled his radio and Fruitcake's M-16 against himself in the bedroll. He took out his eight-inch campknife and stabbed it in the earth by the pistol. The army had given him his pistol and radio but he had to buy the knife and steal most of the other gear he carried or wore. Batteries for his radio he bought from rear-echelon troops by trading them counterfeit N.V.A. belt buckles with those fancy stars on them. Fruitcake's life had bought Waldo his rifle.

He huddled in his bedding and ran his hand across the grass separating him from his slit trench to check the distance he'd have to roll if mortars started coming in. He smoothed back his hair damp with sweat and lay back under a velvet darkness, his nose testing the scents of the earth, water, trees. He listened to the wind. The air felt like autumn after a shower. The trees around him were bare from defoliant. Orion stood low on the horizon. On some distant hill a tiger yowled like a baby crying. Waldo wanted a woman. A woman with laughter and long hair to lie there with him to see and smell and taste everything he could. A woman who could

41

remind him of the man he could now barely recall as being himself, a man who, in some far time and some distant country, had been a better man than the Waldo he now knew. He drifted into bottomless sleep and woke to the scratching of a brushbuck in the deeper trees. He slept again. He woke as another man stumbled into the brush to urinate. He slept.

He woke with a start at the first flash of morning, expecting to see the others awake and crouched against the fearful first light, but he woke from deathly sleep with adrenaline pounding through his heart. He snapped on his pistol belt and radio straps, snatched up his knife and pistol, Fruit-cake's '16, boots laced, maps in pockets, compass swinging on a shoestring from his neck, up and ready for war.

"They're coming for Fruitcake!" yelled the captain, his outstretched arm pointing over the valley of Highway 19, its asphalt squeezed between fields of gray white lettuce and green jungle, two platoons of tracks and tanks racing in from the east, choppers diving from the Mang Yang bluffs west and, centered, an exploding minesweeper tank and another tank like a bedeviled hound dodging and churning past rockets and enemy riflemen and behind them the last dead American tumbling out of the bed of a blasted pickup truck.

"Oh Christ!"

"Drop ya packs!"

"Platoons on line!"

Waldo clicked on his artillery net radio and shouted into the handset, "Yonkers three-one, three-one, this two-four, two-four, firemission, over!"

They plunged off the ridgeline and swept into the forest, hacking at branches with machetes and rifle butts, cursing the jungle, blasting off stray rounds in their frustration and shouting encouragement to the tank — a terrific blast behind the leaf wall — they dived through the brambles shredding clothes, dumping radios, throwing down canteens, and burst into the clearing, screaming, burning, breaking with their bullets — but the tank was slumped and exploding again and again, arcs rising from it in flashes of yellow and green, the gun tube ruptured and cartwheeling into the trees, the turret split open — and the enemy gone! Friends dead! Men fell sobbing in rage. Waldo, with the artillery radio and his rifle slung on his back, phone in one hand and pistol in the other, raised his .45 and fired it into the trees behind which ran the enemy. He fired and fired and fired until the magazine ran empty and the slide refused to close.

Sar'n Mars stood over the body of a dying Arvin grunt whose stumps of legs gouted blood. He had been thrown out of the back of the blasted pickup truck. "He's wasted, poor bastard," Mars reported in a shout. He opened the Arvin's shirt, found his dog tags and tossed them to the only intact member of the Arvin minesweep team, a man staring transfixed by the pouring legs.

Already they were sanitizing the field of battle. The medevac choppers had swooped away the Yank and Arvin bods. In the chopper taking him to the hospital, lifting them both out of war, the dying Arvin watched the last living member of his squad rob his pockets. The wrecker from L.Z. Action had towed the gutted tank out of sight down the road. The G.I.s had neatly stacked the enemy corpses on the road for the villagers to plunder, then shot the bods to pieces with autofire.

"Sar'n Mars!"

"I hear ya, Peepsite."

Peepsite slammed another mag into his '16. "I didn't have nothing to do with this, Sar'n Mars!" He loosened another burst into the enemy corpses and walked away toward the trees.

"I know ya didn't, Peeps."

"I ain't even here."

"That's right. You ain't here often."

The virgin forest was again serene, waiting.

"Let's go!" shouted the captain, motioning uphill with his black-gloved fist.

The Bravos seeped away into the trees, turning their backs on the wreckage that was no longer their responsibility but the women's work of the helis and went up the mountain and over into the Valley.

* * *

It was as though they had never slept, as though they had never eaten. They trudged over Baldy with the bone-weariness of men doing the world's toughest work on the least sleep and food. A soldier is always exhausted, a forest animal forever in the season of starvation. He is poor and ragged. They went into the valley, forty-one weary infantrymen and one redleg, Waldo. The fighting soldiers are despised for fools by the rest of the army, by those too smart to hump or clever enough to pull berths as clerk typists and mechanics or assignments to Europe or Korea. No one in the army loves a combat soldier but another combat soldier. That love is without ordinary expression but sealed with the code that a man will lay down his life for his buddy and his buddy will do the same for him. Bravo tramped into the Valley after the downed chopper to fulfill the code. They could not do otherwise. They could not think to do otherwise.

It was a bright summery morning, the grass green and yellow and only waist-high now. The bushes, leaves, and trees smelled fresh after the night's rain. They cut trail down into the valley across a dozen stream beds and found an enemy trail — while the meadow grass was six inches tall, grass on the trail was worn to bristle and bare red earth. Captain Foley reported the trail to higher as the first gunships rocketed overhead, spinning out over the Valley in the first good light of day searching for their down comrade. These were a mix of Light Observation Helis – Loaches – and Cobra gunships. The small, two-man Loaches acting as eyes for the fierce but blind – because they fly so fast – jet-powered Cobras. They were the air cav from the adjoining Area of Ops, which meant they were under no obligation to Foley. They were infamous for their bad coordination with the ground troops, and they were arrogant about it. The Bravos ducked their heads as these powerful machines swept over.

Cigarettes passed up and down the column. The men were quiet. The flank guards left and right betrayed themselves only by the soft sounds of leaves brushing over cloth and the occasional hack of a machete. The company entered a tangle of briars and came upon a stream with bamboo thick and tall all around. Here they were out of sight of the choppers and felt safer, though Chuck liked to ambush in such places. Foley split the company for security, the first platoon crossing upstream and the second meeting it at the clearing under the canopy of bamboo leaves. All they found were the bones of a water buffalo. The stream was cloudy gray but they filled their canteens, adding iodine, and drank. A brushbuck barked somewhere deeper in the throat of the valley. They pulled south, Sar'n Mars on point. Ants crawled up their trousers from the ground littered with leaves. Crickets chattered. The *caw-caw-caw* of a jungle bird and then the red flash of color as the bird leaped out of the branches. The helis and a Hawkeye pulsed past overheard.

Kansas City beside the captain was nervous because he was a short-timer due to leave the country in six weeks. He was resentful and whined about still being in the field. He blamed Foley for his presence and had begun to nurse a fine hatred for his commander. He swung his rifle from side to side, watching, pushing through the brush wide-eyed with terrified alertness. He knew a soldier has only a finite amount of luck and that drains away too quickly. As the soldier nears his time to leave the war, he has very little luck left to protect him. He should be safe back in base-camp where the captain should have left him. Not out here in these mud-reeking, Chuck-infested boonies where it is too damn easy to get shot all to pieces.

Peepsite with his uneven face looked across at Waldo tramping beside him. Waldo moved in his field slouch straining under fifty pounds of rats and ammo and a Prick-ten radio, Fruitcake's rifle in the crook of his arm and supported by a utility strap over one shoulder, safety on but magazine loaded and chambered. The steel helmet that higher insisted they carry in the field – though no one used them – *bonged* against his shoulders with each stride as it swung on its strap from his pack frame.

Waldo dropped his hand to a thigh pocket, yanked out the plastic map and grease pencil. He checked the map against the trail against the compass swinging from his neck on a bootlace. All corresponded. He sighed and put everything away. He marched another five minutes and did it all again. And did it all day, every day. Sometimes Waldo ducked offtrail, behind a shield of leaves, to study his map. He wanted no Chucks to see the map and shoot him for an officer. For the same reason he wore no insignia of rank and now carried his officer's pistol in his rucksack instead of on his hip. He looked more like any ordinary troopie that way. Again, he swept the map from his pocket, adjusted it to the terrain, snapped open the compass, measured his three directions, nodded to himself, and put it all away, performing like a manic toy machine. The grunts got bored with his show and left him to it. Though sometimes he climbed trees to look for Old Baldy and other points of interest to orientate his map. Watching him climb up there past the snakes and spiders offered a moment's diversion. For Waldo, it was intense work: Captain Foley was a lousy woodsman and would surely get them all lost, choppers overhead to help him or not. Getting Bravo there and bringing them back was Waldo's responsibility. That was how Waldo saw it, from all three directions.

The blue net radio crackled. Foley took the handset from Kansas City. "Oh jeez!" he said, "Pass the word back, Kansas — choppers found the wreck. Give me your map, Waldo." Daddy mused over it, holding the still squawking handset until Kansas City took it from him and, in trembling voice, finished the captain's conversation.

"Air cav says it's down in thick brush at grid 532478. That's here, right?" Foley stabbed a finger at the map.

"Over here, Daddy," said Waldo, snapping on his own arty net radio to report the find to Fire Direction Control at L.Z. Action and to have them plot in defensive fires down there.

"That's two klicks farther south," said Sar'n Mars, glowering at the map, using his limp bush hat to wipe sweat from his bald head. "A day's march in *this* brush, minimum."

Foley blinked his magnified eyes at Mars. "Oh, no — the helis take us down. Three search teams of three each. Bad-Henry, I see something like a clearing ahead of us on the map here. You take the point with B-2, two M.G.s, half a plat and push on ahead and secure it for us. We'll call down the choppers there and meet you there. Don't want to give Chuck too much notice of our presence. Gotta be quick."

"Yo, Captain." Bad-Henry with his troops happy to be shaken from their sun-baked boredom and streaming sweat plunged eagerly ahead on fresh adventure.

"These are the search teams," announced the captain to the thirty G.I.s clustering around him. "Higher wants redleg out there just in case, so Waldo goes. That leaves just eight slots." The foot-sore G.I.s groaned. "One slot goes to B-2 for Waldo, another Sar'n Mars. Sar'n, you take Peepsite and Loopy. The Bee to lead the third team with two riflemen. When we get into the clearing, ditch your packs with your buddies. Sling three bandoliers of ammo apiece. Waldo, I know you don't like hand grenades on your team, so you other teams take three hands apiece. One grenadier — you, Ayrab — go with Waldo. Sar'n Mars and Bee, I only got enough radios to give one to one of you — the other stuff flares in his pocket and see if maybe there's not a loose Prick-ten in the chopper to steal. Got it? Good. Let's move."

They ran into the clearing under the fierce beat of the first chopper's blades — a Huey slick with a machinegunner hanging out each side — and each team piled on board as, one after another, the three slicks dipped into the meadow that was barely fifty meters across and scooped them up. With his company depleted by a quarter, Captain Foley started his remaining thirty-three men to work on foxholes, chopping logs for overhead cover, and setting up mortar pits for the two 60mm mortars they'd brought with them. The 60mm is not authorized issue for a straight-leg company but Foley bought them for his boys, and the ammo, from a top sergeant he'd caught pilfering beer from the basecamp Post Exchange to resell to G.I.s and Chucks in the cathouse he owned. For his freedom, the N.C.O. paid happily with two sixties he stole from a Green Beanie A-Team that had refused to take the field when there were common soldiers to do all that grubby work out there, instead. Then, less happily, he found himself required to continue to supply Bravo Company with mortar ammo for the privilege of continuing to pilfer from the P.X.

Foley let them make cook fires to eat hot food — after the choppers had given away their laager to the Chucks, it made no sense to maintain the strictest security. And there was the air cav overhead to help them if things hotted up. The birds chirped, the crickets sang, deer bolted across their perimeter. They whiled away the hot day listening to transistor radio music from Hanoi. They made a ring of soldiers and weapons just inside the trees – good protection from enemy mortar rounds – guarding the precious little meadow on which the choppers would land to bring their buddies back to them or to extract the rest of Bravo Company, if that were needful.

* * *

Waldo had dived under the rotors of the first slick, its skids jumping on the grassy red earth like a thoroughbred impatient to run, and had barely scrambled on board with B-2 and Ayrab when the machine lurched into the sky, the driver shouting over his shoulder, "We got the redleg back there?"

"That's me," said Waldo.

"You got it plotted?"

"Delta Tangos at the cardinals. They don't want steel now, do they?"

The driver shook his head and peered across the thin blue sky as the slick swooped deeper into the valley. Their guide was the first dead man. A doorgunner had leaped from the falling chopper and was skewered on the tip of a pine tree. Waldo and the others looked out at it in sick revulsion, watching The Bee's team being inserted there to pull him down, thankful it wasn't them.

They were there! "L.Z.'s cold," shouted the driver sitting on his armored seat. "Can't touch down — earth's too soft after rain — good enough for boots — get out!"

The chopper dropped to ten-foot altitude while the machine, afraid of enemy bullets and with the stink of a chopper death in its nostrils, skittered there in the air. "Hey, put us down farther!" shouted B-2.

The pilot shook his head. "No way — this place can hot up all the attention it's getting – I'm not Chuck's meat. Jump!"

Waldo was the first out. As he jumped he saw the wreckage of the downed chopper — a Huey slick with a red cross painted on its tail boom. It was like a crushed grasshopper with only its tail left whole, the rest mashed down into wet earth the color of ash. He tumbled through long, rotor-beaten space, landing on his feet and sinking to his knees in swamp covered with a thin crop of grass. "Hey! Hey!" he shouted up at the black polliwog skittering above him. "Don't jump, you guys! Bring that thing down here!" But it was too late — B-2 was leaping into space. His foot caught on the skid as the heli bounced, he cartwheeled down on top of Waldo, and Ayrab with his M-79 grenade launcher and three bandoliers of snub-nosed grenades fell on both of them. They thrashed around in drowning panic in the sucking mud, too many legs and too many arms, caught there in clear fire from the trees, as the chopper jumped away. They dragged and shoved each other, panting, to hard ground among the tree roots, and watched — as they wiped sweat from faces and mud from weapons — as the third heli sank behind treetops to drop Sar'n Mars's team a klick away.

Waldo put his radio on the company net and reported in: "We're down and see the others down — we're by the wreck and going in, out."

"Let's go," said B-2, scrambling to a crouch.

"I'm huggin' your tail, buddy," said Ayrab. "You lead out, Admiral."

They moved in on the wreck on skirmish line, moving like woods creatures jumpy in hunting season. It took them thirty minutes of noisy and frightening machete work to get through the brush to the chopper. Flight manuals that had been torn apart and the pages thrown up into the treetops when the machine had exploded drifted down around them. They broke into the hillside clearing burnt out by the chopper and stood gawking at the wreck. The tiny rotor on the long tail boom creaked over in an errant breeze. The body of the machine, the great glass and aluminum hull that made it look in flight like a polliwog, had been reduced to ash and all its contents burned up with it.

"I'll stand fast here," said Waldo. "You go left and right around the clearing and recon. Keep in the tree-line but in sight of me and each other."

B-2 and Ayrab moved into the brush. If there were any Chucks around, they were already bushwhacked. At least Chuck would have booby-trapped the wreck. But Ayrab whistled softly the all-clear. They came out of the trees to the wreck.

"Spotted what might be a blood trail over there, leading north-north-east, up toward Sar'n Mars's team," said B-2.

Waldo called Mars to report. Ayrab stared at Waldo to avoid looking at the wreck. "Okay," said Waldo, clicking off the handset of his radio, "let's search this thing and the woods around. Listen for Chuck." Now they both gaped at him, unwilling to look at the horror their mission had brought them to find. Waldo led out. They followed.

It was not much of a search. The fire had left little to sift through. There, in the frame of the cockpit window, on the left side where the co-pilot sat, staring out of the ash at them, was a skull in its helmet. The fire had been quick and hot and had taken everything else, leaving only the protected skull in its armored helmet resting on the armored shield that every pilot sat on. "I never wanna fly in one of those things again," said B-2.

"Then how you gonna get outa here?" said Ayrab.

Waldo said, "Fire burned so fast he was dead before he knew it."

"Some guys got no luck at all," said B-2. "And he was sitting on his armor plate!"

Ayrab loosed a shuddering sigh. "We got none, either. Why couldn't we have found a live one? Who's gonna pick up that skull?"

"Dead is dead," said B-2. "His Mama'll want this." He plucked the helmet from the ash and pried out the skull. Singed flesh and hair stuck inside the helmet, the reek a bitter meat stink. B-2 dropped the mess and ran for the woods, vomiting, falling to his knees with the power of the convulsions. Ayrab turned away to avoid seeing either the skull with its bloody hairy crown or B-2 retching.

50

Waldo unrolled the poncho tied to his pistol belt. He picked up the skull and rolled it in the plastic sheet, looping the roll around one shoulder and tying the ends. He said to Ayrab, "Let's eyeball the woods."

There they found the second thing, stretched out like a figure from Pompeii caught at its moment of death, arms flung out, not even dog tags remaining. They would have kicked through it without recognizing it — crucified ash — but two of the long bones remained, shriveled and blackened, and ten feet farther into the trees was the pilot's helmet with his name on it. Waldo wrote the name in grease pencil on his plastic map, the map more sacred to him than his dog tags, they'd kill him before he'd part with it. B-2 came along, gripping his stomach, his '16 in his free hand. Ayrab unrolled his poncho pack and did as Waldo had done. He picked up the two femurs between thumb and forefinger and rolled them in his poncho. "What do we do about the ash, Lieutenant?" he asked, his face bloodless with the shock of asking the question. He fixed bright glittering eyes on Waldo. "We oughta do something about the ash."

"Bury it," said B-2. "Kick mud over it."

"We'll take it," Waldo said. "Unroll your poncho."

B-2 stared at him, stricken, then unrolled his poncho and laid it by the ash figure.

"I'll do it," said Ayrab. "I already got it on my hands." He scooped up the ash and filled the poncho, his breath coming higher and sharper as he worked. He stood up with shaking hands as B-2 tied the plastic sheet and looped it around his waist. Ayrab shook off the ash and wiped the last paleness on his fatigues and cried, "Let's go!"

But there was the blood trail. It twisted through the brush past the ash figure. Could there be another, a live survivor, crawled back into the brush? Or had a tiger gotten him? They pushed along the blood trail, Waldo calling ahead to Sar'n Mars that they were coming and reporting what they had found.

* * *

The formula for war is thirty days of boredom and thirty seconds of terror from which the soldier slogs back into his numbing boredom. Patrolling was a special bore to Staff Sergeant Mars, and without his mission to see the young men of Bravo trough the war, he would have been content to take what was rightfully his and abandon the war to the young men. After four years in Vietnam, Mars could have any billet he wanted in base-camp, where he could eat, find sex, drink himself into contentment. That was his due. But there was something special that kept bringing him out into the woods: He loved Vietnam.

Not the Vietnam on the map — that place existed on another planet, Uncle Chuckie's planet, a place where the Department of Procurement turned its profits and no place Mars ever wanted to see. No, his Vietnam was the Vietnam of bright, cool country where no man had ever been before, where the tigers had no taste for human blood and where the ground was not polluted with jump-up bombs, where each color was a shade lighter than he'd expected, where the sun was everywhere in thick sheets, cutting, curving, cornering between the forest trees filling all that brisk terrain with flapping, screeching life, pushing out of his mind demon memories of dead men and the family he'd abandoned in Burgerland.

This land he walked had belonged to Frenchmen who lay rotting beneath his tread. He thought of that, too. Yet now, plodding along a trail-less jungle hoping for survivors of the downed chopper, he could not think of them or of death. In the quiet lushness of the forest beneath the old round-shouldered mountains, Vietnam seemed an unlikely place to die. He was clean, healthy, vibrant, virile, terrified, breathing gritless air, shielding his eyes from jungle colors that were clanging bright, the cold ball of ever-present fear above his groin. He was alive in a place that was alive.

Peepsite and Loopy, who had a child's fascination for everything strange, clucked and brought Mars out of his reverie.

"We got movement," Peepsite said in a low voice. He pointed south.

"Waldo's team. Must be," Mars said. They moved cautiously through the trees.

"Hope it *is* Waldo and not Chuck," said Loopy.

Peepsite muttered, "Shut up."

They found Waldo, B-2, and Ayrab staring at the ground.

"Blood trail ends here," said Waldo. "You find anything?"

"Nope," said Mars. "We better check out the surrounds. He's got to be here somewhere."

But they found nothing. No body. No more blood trail. Nothing. Waldo called Captain Foley. "Daddy, we got a dead end here. No bod and the blood trail just peters out, over."

"Look like Chuck, over?" asked Foley.

"If it was, he'd have ambushed the chopper. Not even a booby there. I don't figure it. We checked it out, over."

"Tigers," Peepsite said, scoping the forest in detail.

"Listen," Foley said on the radio, "I got to pull you out of there. The air cav is gettin' antsy. You been in there long enough to attract Chuck. I'll call for your extraction before the air cav finds something better to do with its toys, out."

"But what if he's out there alive somewhere, over?"

"Then he's M.I.A. and I'm sorry for him. But one lost is better than you six K.I.A. We'll try something else but I'm bringing you in, out."

The air cav sent one slick for all three teams, and two Cobras for protection. The men from Bravo piled in with joyous relief. Ayrab sat against the bulkhead, his long-fingered hands ash white, staring white-faced and big-eyed at nothing. The skewered body The Bee had brought down from the tree was sprawled stiffly across the deck. They piled the poncho rolls of bones and ash on the white-eyed corpse to make room for themselves.

The heli jumped away from the L.Z. into the protection of its two Cobras. The pilot, seeing the spoils of the downed chopper, kept higher than necessary by hundreds of feet. The Bravos were ecstatic to be up there out of Chuck's country, if only for minutes, to be safe beyond rifle range, but they were also angry, wrung out, self-hating: They had gone looking for buddies to bring home and found a cruel joke instead. They had failed their buddies. Now one of them was M.I.A. It was as though they each believed that by the power of his good will alone he could save a man's life. They had failed because they were not the superman they had to be.

* * *

"We're goin' in!" yelped Peepsite, his massive frame sitting on the deck of the chopper, his legs dangling out into space. Below them was Captain Foley with Kansas City, in the center of the little meadow, direct-ing the chopper in. Peepsite was the first to be hit: His warped face twisted apart as he took a .30 M.G. round through the head, splattering himself all over the others. He bucked against the bulkhead and then was flung forward into space, arms thrown out, screaming, falling on Foley as the others leaped out of the chopper that was already jumping away from the L.Z. without touching down — the driver wanted to be gone, and the grunts wanted out of that firetrap. They left the remains of the three dead men from the downed chopper in the custody of their own kind, hit the spongy meadow earth tumbling to their feet, grabbing up weapons, radios, Captain Foley and Peepsite, and ran for the tree-line as the second burst of the enemy machinegun fire sizzled overhead, *thunking* through the light aluminum body of the chopper that was shrieking up out of range.

4.

It took the second enemy burst to shake the Bravo perimeter out of its separate reveries of the war's end and to open into the trees a clattering fire sharpened by the earsplitting explosions of half a dozen M-79-launched grenades.

"Incoming!"

"It's a goddamn 82!" shouted Knobs, his bowlegs propelling him into a bunker.

"Inta yer holes!" yelled Mars. They could hear the bangs of the enemy tubes firing — three mortar tubes, close together and close to them — and that meant very high trajectories and that meant they had plenty of seconds to dive for cover while those big 82mm mortar rounds rose out of their tree hideouts, arced up a thousand feet in the clear sky, and then fell at them in a rushing, screaming blur that none of them wanted to hear.

"Damn good gunners!" shouted Waldo. They had Peepsite in their arms in Foley's half-completed bunker — the stink of damp earth and of freshly cut logs topped with the regulation three sandbags carried per man, earth-filled, plastic-woven bags. Peepsite was blown to pieces. One round had gone side-to-side through his face and another had opened his chest. "I'm not copin' very well," he whispered to the captain. "Who says dyin' don't hurt?" Waldo was up and out of the hole running broken-field around the bunkers — he wanted another place to hide, away from death.

"Get in a hole, Lieutenant! The mortars'll be here in two secs!"

A new round of mortar-firing began.

"Where'd those bastards learn to shoot like that?"

"Where'd they get so much ammo?"

The men with the three tiny 60mm mortars ignored the steel seconds away from shattering around them — they were doing their work: Stripped to the waist, sweating and scrambling, yelling around the three circular mortar pits dug down just three feet — that was all the depth they had time to accomplish — with each little mortar on an earth pedestal in the center. They adjusted and fired by the sound of the enemy tubes, their own little tubes sounding puny against the deep-throated discipline of the even firing of the enemy.

"Time's up!" Mars yelled.

The mortarmen dived into their circular pits and the first three enemy rounds blasted into the trees far beyond camp — the G.I.s howling laughter and scorn — the rounds shattering treetops and spinning wood chips and metal fragments like confetti into the open meadow. Foley had done well to put the Bravos in the trees to save them from mortars and rockets, but he had sacrificed the use of their machineguns to do it.

"Chuck hasn't got our range yet!" shouted the mortarmen, leaping up to fire.

The second barrage crashed down.

"Closer, Chuckie, but not good enough!"

"Ya-haaa!"

The mortarmen worked, ignoring zinging bits of tree and metal.

Waldo dived into a half-made bunker full of white-eyed grunts, his radio hand phone clapped to his ear and mouth with two shaking hands as he said calmly — very calmly because he was so afraid and because he knew it would do no good to excite Fire Direction Control in basecamp, it would only slow them down — "Yonkers three-one, two-four, firemission, over...From Delta Tango Alpha, battery in adjustment, three V.C.

mortars, over." The trembling left his hands. The sweat of fright dried on his face. He was doing his work, he was a pro, it would save him from fear. He watched the grunts in the hole with him: One gaped at him wide-eyed, the other ground his face into the red earth wall, praying.

The fight was forty-five seconds old, the third barrage of enemy mortar fire slammed across the base, this time neatly placed in the meadow but still doing no damage, and no Cobras had come in yet, though Waldo knew Foley in the hole with the dead Peepsite had called for gunnies. Sixteen klicks northeast there was a battery of six 105mm howitzers, its gunbun-nies leaping to their breaches with projos, called out of lethargy into the war again, adrenaline pumping, dreaming jungle dreams of their steel cracking open the filthy Chuck armies and saving Yankee lives.

Waldo crouched in the bunker with the two terrified grunts, watching the sweep hand on his watch, the band looped through the pocket of his fatigue blouse with the face turned toward his chest to avoid sun sparkle, counting off the seconds. At the mark of sixty the radio crackled in his ear and the battery's F.D.C. said, "Shot, over."

"Shot, out!" He raised his head from the hole and shouted across the racketing base, "Keep your heads down! We got U.S. incoming!" The grunts cheered.

Now it had begun! The great swinging battering of the enemy he des-pised — he despised Chuck not because he was the enemy or because Waldo had no sympathy for other soldiers thrown into this useless mess of war, but because if he did not kill Chuck, Chuck would kill him and kill the Bravos who were Waldo's responsibility. If there is resurrection of the spirit, Waldo would have none of it if he failed his company. Already his soul was shriveled. He could afford to lose no more of it in failure.

* * *

It had happened on his sixty-eighth day in the war. The chopper on its pad had whined to life. Waldo had dived under the rotors as the grunt colonel, the Batco, gray hair gleaming with sweat, yanked him inside and shouted, "You got redleg now?"

Waldo nodded, clapped his hand to his free ear to block out the rotors and the shouts of gray-haired Colonel Yoden, a man fat like a ballplayer gone to seed. Waldo spoke slowly and loudly into the radio: "Fire all Delta-Tangos for Strongpoint seven north of highway, over."

"Roger," said the radio voice, "Delta-Tangos north SP seven, out."

Waldo peered between his feet at the basecamp falling away beneath the heli. At two hundred feet the air became frigid. The chopper lurched up to get out of enemy small-arms range.

"Shot, over," said the radio.

"Shot, out," replied Waldo. "First redleg, Colonel!" he shouted. The chopper twisted around the low mountains and the Strongpoint came in sight — two tracks and a tank exploding on the road, soldiers diving cowering into the weeds, V.C. streaming back into the trees, enemy rockets streaking over the hills, six more tracks racing down the highway to the fight.

The artillery slammed up huge clumps of earth and smoke in the predetermined defensive targets. It struck again and again, tearing the earth, churning over the running V.C. Waldo jumped to his feet, and the colonel shouted, "Sit down and strap in, you fool!" but Waldo's eyes saw through thick shell bursts, seeking out the scuttling enemy, and he shouted into his handset, "From target bravo, azimuth five eight hundred, add two hundred!" It was lousy targeting procedure, but it would work.

"Roger. Shot, over," said the radio.

Steel burst along the full line of enemy retreat.

"Right on target!" shouted the colonel.

"Add one hundred, repeat!" Waldo yelled into the radio. He saw an image of the guns in basecamp belching clouds of cordite. He felt the long narrow rounds rocket through the gun tubes on tails of gas. He stood behind the guns and saw the shells arc far out over the mountains and descend. Now his eyes in the chopper caught the rounds as the chopper dropped in a ragged, rapid, terrifying sweep onto the ground: He saw the rounds burst up beyond the mountains like corks bouncing up from deep water, curving up beyond the jungle, striking toward the field, falling as Waldo fell in the helicopter, the shells piercing the Earth in great cauliflower clumps of brown smoke, mud, and shattering steel. The chopper touched down. Waldo jumped out and ran onto the Strongpoint: The bunker had been blown apart, the tank and two tracks in flames. Bullets chunked into the earth at his sides. He flung himself down behind an ammo crate as the third battery of rounds *KRUMP-KRUMP-KRUMPED* into the brush, slashing lifting shrieking. He looked over the ammo crate at the cauliflowers of dust and smoke blowing to smog. He was calm again, no longer the frenzy of those first few helpless seconds, into his professional routine, calling radio orders in a calm voice, his eyes searching the field for enemies he had not yet killed.

The first Cobras swooped down over the Strongpoint firing into the trees long streams of buzz-saw minigun bullets, Waldo called cease-fire to the artillery to let the gunships do their work. He saw blood on his hands and on his handset. He jumped to his feet in surprise and saw a naked red foot jutting out from behind the ammo crate that had protected him. A soldier flung out on the front edge of the ruined bunker, sandbags fallen over him, his shirt soaked with blood and bile. Waldo stared at his own clotted hands and understood everything but felt nothing.

He turned back to the road with his red hands upraised and saw a dozen G.I.s groveling in a ditch behind a flaming track. His ears could hear nothing until the soldiers shouted, "It's gonna blow! Get ya butt down!" A sergeant dived out of his ditch for Waldo and threw him down. "Can't you hear? That son of a bitch's gonna blow up!" He rolled Waldo behind the smoldering tank as the flaming track exploded in a giant *WHAM!* blasting its metal sides flat as a ruined card house, kicking the heavy steel deck thirty feet into the air, exploding steel and smoke mushrooming into the pale sky, the deck crashing down onto the rubble and kicking the warped .50 machinegun barrel-first into the mud. "That's Bo Sartain out there," said Waldo, showing the sergeant his red hands. "He's dead."

"Know it," said the sergeant. "With him when it happened."

Waldo became calm, the fear that terrified every minute of his life and kept him alive and threatened to kill him once again under his control. He saw everything with an old man's eyes, as though he had seen it many times before in a long life. He looked back at the little hill that was the Strongpoint with its ruined bunker torn open and Bo Sartain's naked red foot sticking up from the sandbags, and he wiped the blood from his hands and he did not mourn, because he could not afford mourning. Everything was consumed in staying alive.

The G.I.s got to their feet out of the ditch and did not notice what Waldo saw: The thick weed out in the barren field parted and closed, parted and closed, parted and closed, a silent trembling dance. He thought his hearing had left him again but he could pick out the sounds of boots scuffing the hard ground, tanks churning into the woods under the whine of the helicopter fire, the crank and grind of the wrecker on the highway tugging off the ruined tank and tracks. He saw clods of earth gouged up near the soldiers' boots, a breeze whip their clothes, them shouting, "Hey! Hey!" and then the overwhelming rattle of the hidden machinegun's fire, like a hundred baseball bats rapping on a door, and he saw the soldiers throw themselves backwards twisting and screaming in midair, flinging down their rifles, groveling before the weeds that continued to part and close, part and close, part and close.

Bullets kicked past his calves, ricocheted off the hard ground around him, cut through the aluminum track body behind him, spit their gassy tails in his face. He was the only American standing upright in the fire, standing watching the V.C. machinegunner firing bullets at Waldo, the radio-carrying officer marked with the pistol on his hip, the one by the ruined track, the one oblivious to bullets, the one watching the machinegunner trying to kill him. He saw everything and understood everything. He was not afraid. His brain moved at such speed that he could accomplish miracles of leaping and running between the sizzling flights of bullets, but he chose to stand as he was. The frustration, misery, dreariness, confusion, failure of war had stolen his spirit from him. He could live or die, it made no difference to him now. He could be satisfied with either. He would be tormented by either. He understood it all: The war had him. He did not move. He waited without expectation. The bullets came at him.

Waldo believed he survived that moment because he was a zombie who could have his soul back only if he proved himself a good soldier. The Bravos were his trial by combat.

* * *

"Heads down!" Waldo shouted again as the first six rounds of fifty-pound shells crammed with high-explosive rocketed over the little meadow around which Bravo Company huddled, the shells echoing like the high-altitude whir of jet fighters, and blasted into the trees, sending wood and chunks of metal *whip-whip-whipping* through the forest, clanging into trees and stone, billowing cauliflowers of leaves and dust. The overwhelming power of the impacts stunned the enemy gunners and for seconds there was no sound but the last overhead shrieking of a piece of steel flung out on a high arc deeper into the Valley.

Then it started again.

"Those are good gunners," said Waldo. "Good discipline."

"Do it again, Waldo!"

His head barely exposed over the lip of the bunker, a steel pot he had found on it, Waldo said into his handset: "Add one hundred, over."

"Add one hundred, out...Shot over."

"Shot, out. Incoming!" shouted Waldo.

"Right on!"

The enemy battery smashed into the trees over the perimeter, fragments knifing into the sandbags and spilling them, men screaming with fright and wounds and outrage, and then the tremendous rattling *whoosh!* overhead of the six artillery rounds. A cheer rose from the Bravos. The artillery *KRUMPED!* as one impact in the forest. Waldo shouted over the base: "Anyone see the mortar flashes? Anyone got a fix on 'em?" No answer. He scrambled out of his bunker.

He ran into the meadow and fell to his knees by three enemy impact craters. The slope of the crater walls proved he was firing his arty in the right direction, but how far? He used his campknife to find the nosepiece buried under the crater and laid his knife along the crater wall to trace the angle of fall. Chuck was farther out there than he thought – damn!

"Waldo, you fool, run for it!" Sar'n Mars shouted from Foley's bunker, his jungle hat on his head covering the blood that ran down his face from his sliced bald scalp.

"Ain't you got ears, Lieutenant?"

The heavy sizzling downroar of the three enemy 82s burst in his ears — no time to run and he couldn't be caught standing upright — he threw himself flat on the grass, groveling in the red earth. The three rounds cracked down around him, the concussion driving air from the lungs. He gasped like a suffocating man as it threw him into the air and crashed him and his radio back to earth. The rounds had come in and flung up into the air all their metal and rock, harmless to Waldo clutching the grass. Hot metal sizzled in flesh-cutting arcs beyond the impact craters, over Waldo, into bunkers and hiding men.

Waldo ran to the machinegun bunker nearest the mortars and dived into a mass of squirming arms and legs. He yanked the plastic map from his thigh pocket, did his guesstimate and called in to the impatient guns with a coordinate and ordered, "Battery range and deflection spread, over."

"I like that!" cried Mars, crawling bloody-headfirst into the crowded bunker. "Plow up this jungle, Waldo." He sighted down the barrel of the machinegunner's weapon.

"Shot, over!" said the excited F.D.C. radioman, among six others who fought the war with maps and compasses in a sand-drizzling bunker miles away.

"Shot, out. Here it comes," said Waldo.

"Eyeballs and steaks," said the machinegunner, Loopy, at his gunport staring with happy anticipation into the trees. "That's what all we want to see out there, Lieutenant. I don't want Chuck runnin' up here after me."

"Where are the gunships?"

"They'll be along," Mars replied. "This fight's just begun —"

"And they don't like to show until it's just about over."

A barrage of machinegun and automatic rifle fire with the cracking of hand grenades burst from the trees on the east side of the perimeter, blasting leaves and twigs before it. Satchel charges flung against a bunker's gunports blew logs and sandbags into the tree limbs. Mars leaped from Waldo's bunker and raced around the perimeter gathering a grenadier, a machinegunner, and two riflemen. He drove them white-eyed through the chopping enemy fire and had to do everything himself: Set them up in a bunker that could defilade the enemy, concentrate M-79 and M.G. fire in the center of the enemy attack, shout for the 60s to switch fire over there to drop rounds barely inside the tree-line on the enemy. Though the little mortars would be ineffective, cracking open high up in the treetops where their impact fuses caused them to burst, at least their noise and the flung down metal would keep the enemy off balance.

Cobras at last swooped overhead. Mars, now with a radio on his back, switched up to their freak and heard Captain Foley call the Cobras down on the Chuck riflemen, leaving the three enemy mortars for Waldo's artillery to bury.

"Keep firing! Keep yer heads down!" roared Mars. "Gunnies comin' in!" There was no cheer with that announcement, just a grim relief and mistrust.

The Cobras of the air cav with their Loach seeing-eye escorts, darted across the blue sky, jet engines wailing, and lined up one above the other on the instructions of their Loaches and dived in.

"Now ya gonna get it, Chuckie! Ha ha hoo!" yelled a G.I., standing up in his bunker and loosing a magazine into the trees.

* * *

"Dragon two-one! Dragon two-one! I see 'em! Must be fifty or sixty!"

"It's eighty or a hundred, my man! Breaking right!"

"Let's spoil 'em! Whowee!"

"Two-two, climb to one thousand, we'll come in on three-three-oh with left break."

"That's what I'm doing."

"Two-one, rolling in. Get your little butt outta my way, boy!"

"Loach three, orbiting west."

"And keep that little M-16 in your lap this time, Davy Crockett. Don't get in my way."

"Two-one, two-one, this Loach three, I see smaller element a half-klick northeast!"

"What a hunt today!"

"Makes up for the downed chopper!"

"Where are the white hats?"

"West of the clearing. Everything east is our meat!"

"Shut up and shoot!"

* * *

Mars racing along the perimeter froze in half-crouch as he saw the diving Cobras and cried, "Oh my God!" The Cobras, like flying sharks against the blue sky, swung their snouts at the jungle. "Hit the deck!" he screamed, piling into a bunker at the moment he saw tiny orange flickers at the gunships' flanks. Seconds later, the heavy buzz-saw whine of the miniguns. The noisy forest went abruptly silent: The first ship had pulled up steeply, the second had dived in underneath, when the clatter of steel-jacketed bullets rang around his ears, bullets cutting out cones of jungle, hacking through trees, gouging out *American* bunkers, shattering *American* bodies. Wild screams burst from the bunkers.

The dying Knobs wailed, pierced through both shoulders. He staggered up out of his bunker. His bowlegs buckled and he fell dead. The two Cobras swung up and around in great roller-coaster loops, spitting thousands of rounds into the trees and bunkers, each hot shell slicing through the jungle canopy to slam against bunker, sandbag, bone and flesh.

Across the clearing Chucks' screams echoed the Americans'.

Behind him, Mars heard the whine of another rotor and spun around to another gunport to look out as a tiny Loach scuttled overhead, the pilot leaning far out of his plexiglass bubble to spray the perimeter with M-16 fire.

"Please no please no please no!" wailed a G.I. scrambling for the jumpdown hole to run out of his bunker.

Mars grabbed the G.I.'s jacket and hauled him back inside, shouting, "Stay down shut up don't move!"

"Those are miniguns!"

"Stay in here, idiot!"

"Rockets next! They're killin' us!"

Orange flame cracked open in the forest, splashing the enemy guns. Chuck's screams became piercing howls. "Fire out the ports, everyone!" ordered Mars. "Chuck's running!"

"Am I on fire?" asked a G.I. standing on the jumpdown hole. His hair was blazing. Mars wrapped the man's head in his own fatigue jacket and threw them both on the ground as rifle fire *zinged* over the meadow.

In the center of the meadow, with his R.T.O. groveling in terror at his feet and B-2 on one knee bodyguarding, stood Captain Foley, his steel pot thrown back on his head, his shirt drenched in Peepsite's blood, holding a purple smoke marker in one hand, his other fist thrust into the air at the Cobras, shouting, "You bastards!" The last of Chuck's fire took him.

B-2 screamed, firing his '16 in magazine-long bursts, changing mags as he ran, spraying G.I. bunkers, spraying up at the Cobras, plunging into the fire-gutted and meat-stinking enemy forest with his rifle on go-go, screaming oaths, and he ran into the last steel rain from the Cobras and was torn to pieces. The Cobras vanished from the sky.

* * *

The prevailing westerly breeze blew the gunsmoke from the meadow, along with the bitter taste of cordite and the stink of burned flesh. "Cease firing!" shouted Bad-Henry, now in command. He strode across the meadow ignoring the last Chuck fire and rolled the captain's corpse off the cowering Kansas City. "Get up, Kansas, call us some dustoff, then get me batt."

"Yezzer!"

"Mars! You alive?"

"Yo, Lieutenant! Over here."

"How's your radio?"

"Working."

"Check troops. Casualty and ammo list. Fast."

"Yo!"

"Waldo!"

The artilleryman climbed up out of his bunker, the hand phone still clamped to his dirty face as he ended his firemission. "Here, Bad."

"Tell your higher I figure it was two companies come at us, the cowards wouldn't've used less. Tell 'em I want the D-Ts ready for firing asap on my command."

"Rog."

"Bee! Knobs!"

"Knobs is dead," said The Bee, getting to his feet inside the tree-line. He wasn't about to make himself a mortar target there in the clearing with Bad-Henry. He was pasted with mud stuck over with leaves, more burst sun blisters draining over his face.

"Okay, everyone — stand fast. Eyeballs and ears peeled forward. We get us some slicks in here and we're goin' home." Sar'n Mars came into the clearing. "What's the bad news, Sar'n?"

"Twenty-one effectives, Lieutenant." Mars had a green bourbon-soaked handkerchief clamped to the bloody gouge on his bald head.

"Christ. We lost that many? We're destroyed!"

"Seven K.I.A., four in the bunker that got blown plus Knobs and B-2 killed by choppers. Plus Daddy. Twelve wounded — including all the mortarmen —"

"I'll put those bastards in for the B.S., you know."

"— and most of them a credit to the Cobras."

The lieutenant gazed around him in helpless fury, the tic coming onto his lips without the usual prompting of a smile. "What we got left for armament?"

"Lost one M.G., that's all, and one radio."

"I'd rather have a radio than an M.G." Bad-Henry spat on the earth. "Tighten up the perim and hunker down. Ought to have them dustoff in a minute and right behind them the slicks to get us out of here. What say we have a look out there in the trees."

"We oughta do that but it's damn dangerous."

"Rather lose a patrol now than lose a chopper later and have those fly-boys tell us we're on our own and can hump out."

"Right. I'll go."

"Naw, I need you. You stay. Gimme three gunmen. Tell the troops I'll keep in radio contact with you and they're to ask your permission before firing, just in case it's me they want to blow away. Do my best to keep in visual."

"They mighta dumped some boobies out there."

"I'm careful. Do somethin' decent with the corpses, Sar'n." Bad-Henry trudged off to sling on more bandoliers and a radio and went into the woods with his gunmen.

"Dig yaselves in!" Mars shouted to the company. "We might have a wait. Bee, ya got graves registration duty. Pile the bods someplace safe."

Waldo squatted just inside the tree-line, plotting more defensive targets on his map and calling them in to F.D.C. Mars squatted next to him, pouring more bourbon from his canteen onto his army-issued handkerchief and bathing the still-running wound on his scalp.

"F.D.C. says dustoff on the way, Sar'n, and they put up another stick of Cobras to protect them," said Waldo.

"Not those same two from the air cav?"

"Naw, these're *our* Cobras, the Crocodiles."

"Peep's dead, ain't he?" asked Mars.

"Far as I know."

"So that's eight K.I.A. Well, he's finally not here. Got hisself outa this war. Good luck to him wherever he is."

"You been in this valley before, right?"

"Like I was born here."

"What's the best way out?"

"North. Way we came in. What you thinkin'?"

"I'm thinking we're in the wrong place at the wrong time," said Waldo. "I'm thinking it's curious that your Batco sent this company at night to look for a downed chopper. He ought to have waited for dawn. Send out choppers and have them put a rescue team on the ground when they spot the wreck. That would be S.O.P. It's curious your Batco's about to rotate home and not got his Legion of Honor yet."

"What's that mean?" said Mars.

"Maybe he wants us to buy it for him."

Mars stared back into the woods. "I seen a lot of trash in this war and I seen that once or twice. Who's the enemy in this part of the Valley?"

"The N.V.A. Yellow Division and the 95-Bravo Chuck Regiment, plus some ragtag elements."

"Lotta guys."

"Could be five thousand."

Mars groaned. "We know where they are — the regimental command posts, anyway?"

"A few identified. But we don't like to come into this valley so most of them are anybody's guess."

"You could do that, couldn't you?" said Mars. "Infiltrate one company down here in the dark, mark 'em by sendin' choppers in to 'em, and let that company attract whoever's nearby. Decoy work."

"Then you send in four-five batts with some good arty support and gunships and stir up a real fight," said Waldo. "Rotate home in a blaze of glory, wouldn't you?"

Mars chuckled thinly. "Ya could, ya sure could. I think we've done our share for the colonel's glory, though. Even he knows it's time for us to go home. He'll get us out. We'll be sleepin' in basecamp cots tonight."

"Or it could be," said Waldo, "Chuck will let those three dustoffs in and out because he wants to see us go home and leave him alone down here. When he finds out we're still here, he's not gonna like it. *If* we're still here."

"Sar'n Mars!" shouted Kansas City, cowering in the meadow by the captain's corpse. "Dustoff!" He pointed at the first of three medevac slicks dropping from high altitude searching for the meadow.

Mars ran into the clearing and broke open a purple smoke. "Get those wounded over here fast!" he shouted to The Bee. The first chopper had barely touched skids to earth when The Bee's crew began lifting the moaning wounded onto the deck of the slick. The helicopter was off in fifteen seconds. They did it twice more and evacked a dozen W.I.A. and the stack of eight dead. The air was suddenly peaceful without the cracking of the rotorblades. The sky was empty.

"Where's the ships comin' for us?" The Bee asked.

"Batt," interrupted Kansas City, thrusting the handset at Mars.

Mars listened with tightening lips, said, "Roger, out," and gave the phone to the R.T.O. "We stay put. They're sendin' in Action Company to join us if they can do it before dusk." ·

The Bee grabbed the mike from the R.T.O. and held it out to Mars. "Tell 'em we gotta get outta here! Tell 'em they've pinpointed us for Chuck with dustoff! Tell 'em what'll happen to us tonight!"

"They know all that. That's why they're sendin' in Action."

"But us, a third of a company, and Action against what the Chucks got in this valley — a division and a half?"

"Higher knows it." Mars glanced at Waldo still squatting there in the safety of the tree-line with his map and radio, the eyes beneath that jet black hair stricken now: He had known what was coming but he had not wanted to believe it.

Lieutenant Bad-Henry came out of the trees shouting for the perimeter not to shoot him. He and the others had mud and bloody gunk on their boots and trousers. They'd brought back a few souvenirs — a brass V.C. belt buckle, two AK-47 automatic rifles, and some satchel charges the company could use itself. He said to Mars,

"I heard it, Sar'n, on the radio. What's batt think it's doing?"

"We're winning the colonel his Legion," said Mars, his voice vacant.

"Hope he spreads around some of his glory." Bad-Henry glared into the trees, squared his baseballer's shoulders, bit his twitching lip.

Waldo came out of the protection of the tree-line to join them. "When Chuck realizes we didn't abandon this base in those three dustoffs, he'll come down here again and the slicks aren't going to extract us when he hits. One way or the other, we're stuck here by our lonesome all night. I say we move out now while we can to a new laager and dig in. When night falls, we move out again and set up ambush-style, no holes, and be ready to fight and run north if we have to."

"You're thinking like a redleg, Waldo," said the lieutenant. "You guys can do that runnin' off and guerilla stuff, but Action Company depends on us to hold this L.Z. for them to land here."

"Action isn't coming," said Waldo. "Once Chuckie hots up this L.Z., no slick will dare land. We're on our own and we better think of ourselves first and now."

"Waldo's right," said Mars.

Bad-Henry looked around him at his troops huddling in their bunkers, cutting new covering logs, digging deeper holes. "Right or not, we got orders. We're stickin'. Gimme that." He snatched the handset from Kansas City and called battalion. "We got us a real tight situation here. Recommend if you don't figure to put in here what you promised, you extract us asap, over...Roger that. I got your orders. But it's real tight here and ain't much daylight left. We may not be able to keep this L.Z.

cold much longer. Recommend you get us out or them in within thirty minutes, over...Roger, out."

"What'd batt say?" demanded Mars.

"Told us to sit tight. Sar'n, plan us a bugout route. Pick a prospective laager somewhere north. If Action isn't here by dusk, we move out. Chuck knows where we're at and he's getting himself some more 82 ammo. Waldo, plan some fires along the route Mars picks and some D-Ts at the site. Mars, find something that looks good on the map with maybe rocks or rough ground so we hunker down without digging holes. I don't want our entrenching tools chunking all night telling Chuck where we're at. Bee, you got what's left of first plat and all the guys on the eastern half of the line. Find Pinball and tell him he's got the western perim."

With his dispositions made, Bad-Henry led Kansas City, shaking with short-timer's nerves, into the safety of the tree-line. Together they squatted over a stove punched out of a C rat can and used a bit of C-4 plastic explosive pinched off Bad-Henry's five-pound bar to cook their first hot meal in twenty-two hours. It was 1800. Dusk filled the horizon and the space between the trees.

A half hour later Chuck, uncertain that all the Yanks had been withdrawn on just three helicopters, probed the perimeter and took two wounded for his trouble. Bad-Henry had to report that to battalion headquarters. The slicks refused to come into a tiny jungle L.Z. that was hotting up, especially when there was a division and a half of Chucks down there and absolutely no element of surprise. The pilots had the image of the downed chopper in their minds, too. The Batco went with the flyboys: The expenditure of another twenty-odd men – not counting the redleg who came from the artillery battalion and wouldn't be the Batco's responsibility if lost – was better than losing a string of choppers and all of Action Company. That was no way to get his Legion. Besides, he was infantry and he liked to watch the infantry fight.

Night fell. Bad-Henry had lost the company's chance to escape by itself. Chuck began to probe the thin perimeter.

5.

This is how the night went: First, there was a stirring in the soul that seemed to each soldier either fear or courage but was both. Second, there was the screaming that would not stop. Third, there was the dying.

The Bee on the eastern perimeter, with eight men in two-man foxholes and Sar'n Mars breathing down his neck, watched evening slide up and thought if his failed suicide attempt had not shown he would survive this war, he would be dying tonight. As evening darkened, The Bee sent a few men sliding out through the broken weed to set out the claymore mines – like Polaroid cameras full of ball bearings and plastic explosive. He adjusted the bipod on his M-16 and set it in the bunker's gunport. He shivered with exhaustion, the cold sweat soaking his fatigues, the evening chill, and no food. He pulled his camouflaged poncho liner around his shoulders. His fingers trembled, they trembled in every fight. He wondered if they would always tremble, if he could not stop them trembling. If back home in Burgerland sitting in a burger shop years away from the war raising a Coca-Cola to his mouth his hand would tremble so much he would spill it on his face. Worse, if it would happen so often he would not notice. The moon tried to rise, he cursed it to blackness. No breeze — good!

Lieutenant Bad-Henry crawled into the bunker and passed The Bee and Mars the Starlight scope to survey the woods in its green electronic lens. "You don't see any goddamn rocket launcher, do you?" Bad-Henry demanded.

"Nope," said The Bee, concentrating on the green view of the woods. "If they was out there, their sights would pick up this Starlight's radiation pretty quick and I'm dead."

"Got to risk it," said Bad-Henry. "This thing's the only edge we got." He crawled out to finish his rounds of the foxholes.

The machinegunner behind his M-60 began to snore standing up at the gunport. The Bee was astonished and outraged, he jostled the gunner awake. In the pale fluorescence of the stars, The Bee under his poncho liner looked like a mound of earth. For an instant he felt unfindable and unkillable. He continued his preparations for the night calmly, as though he were back home, deer hunting. He thought about the woman in Denver, about lying between her warm thighs as autumn stiffened the grass and trees shed leaves as carelessly as that sexy woman shed her clothes. Would a woman stay faithful to a soldier gone to war? Would she still wear his ring when he got back? He laughed at the stupidity of his thoughts, like a jukebox full of sentimental songs. His fatigues felt cold. He was surprised to find them drenched with sweat. Blood moved painfully through his cramped arms. His eyes ached with the effort of searching the unmoving forest for that slight jerk of motion that would betray Chuck.

"There they are!" Mars shouted. "Fire!" Claymores *whooshed* alive, their pellets gouging up earth. Machineguns, rifles, grenades — Chuck was gone! The forest still again! Orange-red tracers zinged across the night. "Stop it, stop it! Cease fire!" shouted Mars.

The Bee's throat was choking him, jammed with fear, his weapon smoked, the bitter stink of cordite gagged him. He forced himself to slide back into the combat routine of watchful anxiety. He watched everything at once and quietly, unmoving, like a trapped animal, brushing from his

74

mind every thought but a Chuck-scenting concentration. The trembling left his hands.

Sergeant Mars crawled down the line to check for wounded and returned with the news that two of The Bee's men lay dazed and staring at the sky, their ears blasted from the concussion of their own mines placed too close to their position. They'd been too afraid of Chuck to string out their claymores the proper distance into the trees.

Green enemy tracers streaked level and flat from the forest! *Yellow blast of a grenade!* Tinkling fragments showering down, The Bee's ears minutes behind his eyes, yellow still shrieking across his face, his ears ringing with the grenade burst, he squirming deeper into the earth, pulling his trigger in long bursts filling the black before his eyes with red fire, screaming, "Cease fire, cease fire!" and meaning it for Chuck, but his own men ceased firing and so had Chuck. Quiet. His finger snapped away from the trigger. He vomited out the gunport. He sucked breath. He glanced over at Sar'n Mars: His face was caved in. The grenade had him. "Great God, Sar'n Mars, are you dead?" he cried. The machinegunner gasped and fell back against the wall. Mars's corpse rolled backward with a wheeze that said, Yessss.

The Bee put a blank expression on his face and stared into the black night. He had no more thoughts of the woman in Denver. He picked up Mars's radio handset and called Bad-Henry. "Mother Hen is dead," he reported.

* * *

Waldo carried many fears but his worst was the fear of mortars. It was natural for an artilleryman to fear most the weapons he used himself. Waldo listened for them as he ran across the tiny meadow, he knew they would be silent. He watched, he knew he would never see their muzzle flashes. His ear insisted it heard the distinct *bang* of an 82! No, no, no, that was crazy. He expected to turn his head and see yellow blasts! To feel pounds of steel clanging through his skull! To jump and run and have

75

his legs and arms hacked away, his headless corpse gushing blood. He expected to see mortars burst once in unison and then work quickly over their base in professional jumps, first out and then in and away, following each running man into his ravine and bush, scouring his ragged flesh, smashing at his bones. He wanted to run, to scream, to cry for mercy. His body jerked and shook. He searched for the yellow flashes among the black trees. He pulled out his campknife to defend himself against the mortars and then he knew that he was going mad and his fear would kill him. He stood in the meadow and laughed in howls. He willed calm onto his face, the effect seeped into his brain. He must be cool to live. He did not struggle to be calm, he simply turned off his brain. He refused to think. He let his body survive independently on its senses. He dived for The Bee's bunker. *A yellow burst!* A crash like a door slamming in an empty house! Grenade pieces blasted past his ears, Fruitcake's M-16 was shattered and torn from his grip.

He clapped the handset to his head and shouted over the screaming of the new-wounded and the machineguns' roar. "Firemission, firemission, firemission!" He was on his knees screaming fire orders into the phone, red tracers coursing away from the perimeter and green tracers zipping up at him, he had only his knife in his hand, he was hysterical.

"Target India, battery two, fire fire fire!" The terrain in front of him expanded, glowing swooping outward, metal and dirt and rocks spattering over the G.I.s, their rifles and machineguns blasting long orange streaks into the yellow light as they cheered and howled. He fell on his face over-joyed.

"There! There! Over there! Watch my tracers!" The Bee shouted from his bunker and the line swung its weapons' fire onto three dark running figures.

"Running V.C.!" Waldo shouted into his radio. "Repeat! Repeat!" He grabbed up a grenade launcher he found lying there. "Add five-zero, fire for effect!" he howled. He was so terrified he loosed one round after another from the grenade launcher, snatching up snub-nosed grenades from bandoliers strewn on the ground, firing the next round before the previous had impacted. There in the stark forest lit by the bursts of his grenades the artillery exploded again and he watched the Chucks throw out their arms and weapons and be swept away by cannon fire and by machinegun fire and their remains ground down by his last grenade.

He found himself on his knees again. He heard the screaming again. The last artillery bursts did not blot it out. The grenadier whose weapon he held lay face down on the bunker lid screaming into the ruptured sandbags. Waldo rolled him over and the screaming stopped as the man died. Green tracers crisscrossed in front of Waldo. He flung himself off the bunker and into the jumpdown hole, dragging with him two bandoliers of grenades from the grenadier's corpse.

"Shout 'comin' in' before you dive into a man's foxhole, Waldo, you scared the daylights outta me!" yelled The Bee's machinegunner as he faced front to watch the silent black woods, the screams of Americans and Chucks echoing in the trees.

"We'll have Spooky on-station in an hour," said Waldo. "He's in a fight over in Pleiku right now."

"Lotta good that'll do us when we'll all be dead by then," said The Bee.

"What's your casualty count here?"

"Three, best I can tell, all wounded but still shooting. Sar'n Mars is dead."

"Dead grenadier on the roof of this bunker. I didn't see his face," said Waldo. "Take my '16 ammo." He unslung it and looped it over a stub of log supporting the roof. He patted Mars on the shoulder. "That had to be fast."

"Didn't feel it," said The Bee.

The machinegunner stared resolutely into the trees. "Quiet now," he said.

Another battery of defensive targets roared into the trees, raising to a high skittering screech the wails of the Chuck wounded out there.

"It's quiet – good time to check the line." Waldo crawled up out of the bunker and low-crawled north through the battle-littered stubble of grass to the next bunker. "This is Waldo up here," he said, remembering the machinegunner's warning. "Who we got down there?"

"Waldo! We just about shot your tail off. Whistle or something next time you crawl around a man's position."

"Anybody hurt?"

"I'm Ayrab and I'm okay. We got a M.G. and it's okay, too. The Hardluck Kid's with me. He's in shock or something. Hates bunkers and we took a grenade on top. That did him."

"Don't know what to do for that. Here, take this — all I got." Waldo handed Ayrab a metal flask of vodka. "Don't get smashed. Ya got work to do." Waldo crawled away.

Ayrab took a fastidious first suck. He was hyper enough that he could drink it all without effect. He pried open the Kid's lips and forced the vodka down his throat, slapped him and gut-punched him, and the Kid came around. "Christ, it happened again, didn't it?" the Kid yelled.

"Nothing happened again. Drink some of this. It's officer's booze and it'll make ya big and strong. Drink. Waldo's orders."

The Kid drank and his eyes cleared. He said calmly, "Ya ever seen a rocket come into a bunker?"

"Naw, and I never want to."

The Hardluck Kid was Private First Class Curry, assistant gunner on Ayrab's machinegun. He had a pale girlish face that made him look, when he went into one of his trances, like a marble child. Around his neck with his dog tags he wore a silver crucifix given him by his mother, but because silver sparkles in sunlight and moonlight he had wrapped it in black electrician's tape. He often worried that the tape covering might diminish the power of the cross. He wiped sweat from his trembling chin and rested his hand on the M.G. as they both peered out over their assigned field of fire. "There was twelve of us in this bunker and a couple of boom-boom girls," said the Kid.

"I don't want to hear it," said Ayrab.

"It was a first-rate bunker, on Bridge 25, and one B-40 come in. It went through eighteen inches of sandbagging like window glass. It went through three twelve-by-twelves holding up the roof and buried itself half-way through the sandbag wall on the other side."

"I told you – I don't want to hear this!" cried Ayrab.

"While it was doing all that, it threw off so much energy and sent things zapping around inside that it was like a egg-beater got in there. I was standin' in the doorway when it hit. Threw me down, God damn threw me down – look how big I am and it threw me down. I got up and found all of them like goo, the guys and the girls altogether just goo, like some-one had been smashing tomatoes on the walls in there. That's all was left of 'em."

"I tell you again I don't want to hear it," said Ayrab, angry, "you don't tell it to me again, roger?"

"I had the hard luck to survive and see all that."

"Makes me wanna be sick," said Ayrab, staring out into the woods where the continual *KRUMP!* of the defensive arty fires continued. "Makes me want Chuck to come up here so I can kill something."

"You were one of 'em found the downed chopper, weren't ya?" said the Kid. "That any different?"

"Not like that, wasn't like that, God damn it." Ayrab looked at his hands, still seeming so ash-white to him, and trembling again. He put them on the M.G. "I really am gonna be sick if —" There was Chuck! "Those Mikes got satchel charges!" Ayrab clamped his finger on the M.G. trigger and cut them down.

"They got rockets! They got rockets!" screamed the Kid, scrambling for the exit.

"Naw, naw, naw! Just satchels!" Ayrab shouted over the clatter of his gun. An M.G. opening fire was the prime target Chuck's rocketmen were looking for. The B-40 rocket went into the gunport whizzing past Ayrab's ear just as the Hardluck Kid scrambled out into open air. The bunker and Ayrab ballooned up out of the earth, carrying the Kid with them into the meadow, where he lay stunned, his back broken, his legs twisted at bad angles, until the fight was over and he died at last, free of the memory of the last time he didn't die.

Waldo, at the north end of his eastern perimeter in the last foxhole, leaped up, firing grenades into the breach left by Ayrab's M.G. and was astonished to find an enemy squad there rushing in over the bunker's rubble — how did they get through his arty fire? — but they ran past him screaming like fear-maddened animals running from the continual hail of steel and then they were standing gawking around in the tiny meadow and a dozen rifles sent orange tracers crisscrossing through their bodies and pieces of them blew off and they pitched over dead.

The last dying Chuck fell on Lieutenant Bad-Henry where he lay in the meadow as the central point from which to use his Starlight scope to direct rifle and grenade fire at the Chucks infiltrating through the woods. Bad-Henry pushed off the groaning body and stuck his bowie knife into it and it shrieked and died, unnerving him, and he stuck it again. "Chucks bringing in rockets!" he shouted to the line. "Keep a-watch!" He glanced down at his wristwatch's luminous dial strapped face down through the pen slit in his fatigue jacket: 0300. Mother! Dawn in two hours. This was going to be a near-won thing. The luminous time on his watch dial burned into his vision. Would he ever forget all of this and, in his old age, remember only that moment peering in fright at his watch dial held three inches from his nose? A hell of a stupid thing to remember, he thought. But better than remembering Peepsite being torn to pieces there as he fell from the helicopter when the search teams returned.

He lay there sprawled in the clatter and roar of the artillery fire coming in, the racketing of machineguns and grenades momentarily overwhelmed by the *whooshing!* explosions of the arty, and dreamed of the future. But it was a warped future, a frightening future in which he found himself living a half-life of aspirin and orange juice. Going to work in the truck tire retread shop – the only work he could find in the hard economic times before the war, the only work he would expect to find after the war – in a doped aspirin haze. Sliding his roughened hands around the rough bags as he pulled them over the big truck tires and lifted them into the cooking racks. He would go home, take out the gunstock oil and some old rags and rub the oil into the table-sized slab of black walnut he had in the living room of his rundown three-room house. In the kitchen he had the half-welded pieces of wrought iron for the table legs and his wife wanted them out of there. He would fill the rag with oil and run his hands over the sleek wood, rubbing in the oil, and the evening would pass and he would avoid thinking. His wife would watch him, as she always did before the war, from the doorway of the kitchen and be happy that he was calm, at least until the night took him when the torments of war that bubbled in his brain even now would be worse because he could not escape into the fury of combat. An odd escape.

What was that he was thinking – the past or future or something in between or sideways? No, what troubled him now and what he knew would haunt him into that calm future was knowing that he had failed the men he was supposed to lead. He had not bugged out when he had the chance. He had not violated orders and gotten them home safe and later covered up by lying about violating orders in a war that was all lies. He had stayed here as he had been told, and now the only thing in this awful place that was a not lie – Bravo Company – was going to die. They were trapped.

Bad-Henry jumped to a crouch in the meadow, hauling his radio on his back and the Starlight on his M-16 in his hand. He had used the scope too long from one position and if Chuck had some Starlights of his own or even a good perceptive gunner on a B-40 tube with Russian sights — and not the usual bamboo poles Chuck used for launching his rockets — then they'd have Bad's logger and range and they'd kill him next. Bad-Henry thought of that too late. Too late was his constant failure. Two heavy .30 AK-47 rifle rounds came zipping green at him. The first took him in the pelvis and he screamed as it spun him and he grabbed to see if he had any balls left as the second smashed into the radio on his back — the radio saved his life — and threw him forward into the soft earth as it burrowed into his back and stopped behind a lung. He lay screaming a long time before he realized he only thought he was screaming — he hadn't the breath to scream, the pain was so great. Blessed shock flooded out of his system like dope, covering the pain and giving him the euphoria of the dying. Not so bad, he thought, not really that bad. He was thankful. "I'll never see my wife!" he said aloud to himself in his dying dream, and he passed out.

"Bad's got it!" came the piercing panicked wail.

"The company's bought it!" screamed Kansas City, standing over the body. "Where's Waldo? Who's left alive? Am I the only one?"

More artillery blasted down on schedule. Waldo came out of the dusty murk on the meadow. "He's still breathing. Help me get him under cover, then pass the word I'm in charge and *you* tell The Bee — wherever he is. Got it?"

"Yezzer!" They stripped the ruined radio from Bad-Henry and found his second wound, dragged him to his command and control bunker and left him down there with their one rifleman-medic, Cobb, who looked like he'd just been born, he was that covered in blood, his hair and bushy mustache plastered to his skin with the stuff.

"Pinball!" Waldo yelled over to the next bunker to the grenadier corporal in there. "I'm C.O. now! Check the line for wounded, for ammo, and head count – get your butt back here to me in thirty secs!"

"Yo!" Pinball with speed made of terror scrambled out of his dugout to crawl down the line.

"We're all gonna die tonight, aren't we?" said Cobb out of his blood-spattered face.

"Old soldiers don't die, the bastards just fade away," said Waldo.

"We ain't old soldiers," said the medic.

Waldo clapped his arty net handset to his head and said, "Yonkers three-one, this two-four, we're buggin' out of here. All the blueleg oscars are dead or wounded and I'm in command. I don't talk to blue net anymore, just to you. Got that? Over."

"Bug out, you in command, got it, over!"

The drone of a slow-flying twin-engined C-47 aircraft came down to them. It had twin gatling guns mounted in its sides and could put a bullet a second in each square foot of ground for enough acres to fill up Texas. "We got Spooky overhead," Waldo said into the radio. "You tell him to hose down these coordinates, and I'm giving 'em to you in shackle" — he fumbled through his mimeographed codebook to encode the map coordinates — "and then tell him I want him to hose down everything between my laager here and those coordinates along azimuth four-six hundred, got it? Over...Next, at my command fire all Delta Tangos simultaneously, over...Next, at my command put steel on my location, over...Right on, I said on my laager — we'll be gone when I call for it — don't argue, you ain't out here, over...Forget the corpses, I'm going to save live ones. Steel on my laager, out."

Pinball tumbled into the bunker dragging a captured satchel charge behind him. His shaggy hair was pasted to his scalp with sweat and mud.

"What's the bad news?" said Waldo.

"We got ten effectives on both sides of the perim and six W.I.A., two of 'em can't walk."

"Cobb," Waldo said to the medic, "get all wounded in the northern bunker. We bug out from there. Take two men to help you. You got ninety secs."

"Roger!" The medic dived out of the bunker into the rack and roar of the still incoming artillery fire, diving under the green flames of enemy tracers.

"Pinball, send one man to tell The Bee we're bugging out and to rally his men on the northern bunker in two minutes. You do the same. Move out." Pinball leaped up into the violent night and was gone.

Waldo spoke into his hand phone: "Yonkers three-one, two-four, bugout in five minutes. Tell Spooky to go to work. Fire all Delta Tangos, over."

"Spooky, Delta Tangos, out!"

Waldo stripped the unconscious Bad-Henry of everything useful, looping the lieutenant's ammo bandoliers on top of the grenade bandoliers Waldo was wearing, and slinging his M-79. He picked up Bad-Henry's M-16 with its Starlight scope, slammed home a fresh thirty-round mag. He took from Bad-Henry's pockets his hand grenades – Waldo hated the things, they always went off by themselves – pulled their pins and rolled them out the gunport to explode in the confusion of the forest. "Dog tags!" he said aloud. "I forgot the tags!" He ran out of the bunker and in the moments left to him ran crouching over the men crawling to the assembly point and yanked the second tag from each corpse and pocketed it. Then he ran north across the meadow through a crazy warp of green tracer shouting into his mike, "All Delta Tangos azimuth four-six hundred cease fire! Spooky to move north, over!"

"Delta-tangos four-six hundred cease fire — Spooky north — roger, out!"

Waldo fell to his knees with the Bravos huddled behind the northern bunker. "We got all the wounded?"

"Some of 'em are gonna die before we get a hundred yards," said the medic.

"Then you take their tags and leave 'em when they die. Spooky's plowing up a new laager for us. We follow his red fire and when he stops shooting, we're home. Got it? We leave no wounded. Got it?" The arty fire to the north broke abruptly. The black night there, clouded with smoke and dust was suddenly still. "That's the yellow brick road. Bee, you're the tailgunner. Nobody fire unless I say so. We don't want Chuck to see us out there. Let's go!"

Waldo led out on the point with Bad-Henry's '16 in one hand and his radio handset in the other. They stumbled into a gouged-up shattered world of choking dust and bitter cordite reek, the trees shorn of leaves and branches and standing stark stripped white against the black sky and dust-clouded stars, the earth underfoot bleeding black water and full of jagged metal biting into their boots. Men stumbled and fell, lacerating hands, crippling knees. The wounded began to scream and Cobb, with no more morphine, gagged them. They plunged on. Behind them enemy fire into their old base increased to a rolling roar. Chuck was suspicious: No orange tracer was coming back at him.

The Bravos crossed the cratered moonscape that had been Waldo's adjusting point for a defensive target — a churned-over nightmare cleared in the heart of the forest — and followed the red rain of Spooky's gatling gun and the drone of his two engines. They stumbled on another few hundred meters and Waldo called for the northern Delta Tangos to be fired behind them to keep the base ringed in steel to keep Chuck out of it and to prevent his knowing the Bravos had escaped. But Chuck was a tough and wily fighter: A burst of green tracers rose up from the center of the meadow like Chuck raising his triumphant flag over their bunkers and the corpses of their buddies.

As the remnants of Bravo Company pushed forward, Waldo dropped to one knee and called in: "Three-one, two-four, fire on our loggersite, over...Yeah, yeah, we're all out. Just fire the damn thing, out."

More triumphant green tracer bursts arced up over the old base as Chucks crowded into the meadow to howl victory. Then the curtain of steel descended in a yellow *whooshing* roar just as The Bee at the end of the column passed Waldo, who stood transfixed, watching the shells pulverize the meadow and the Chucks. The Bee turned to stare beside him as the rest of the Bravos with their wounded ran toward the slopes of Old Baldy, where Spooky sprayed red fire.

They burst out of the trees running upslope, gasping and stumbling, as the first brassy haze cracked open the night horizon. There in the east, leaping up black and sleek against the dawn, were six Cobra gunships and a long stick of slicks. They were going to get out alive!

But they looked upslope to where Spooky's gatlings had cleared a highway of blackened, withered trees and stared into the eyes of the 95-Bravo Chuck Regiment. The regiment had been sliced through the middle by Spooky but, like good soldiers, they'd stood their ground to wait patiently for Bravo Company. Wounded as they were, they were more a regiment than Bravo was a company. Bravo realized that the long stick of slicks and gunships leaping up against the rising sun was not coming to save them but to bring a regiment of Yanks against this regiment of Chucks on the hill.

It was like the hand of the Chuck god sweeping the hillside clean. All the Bravos on the hillside were washed away in the single blazing roar of the enemy regiment. Waldo groveled in the dirt. The Bee was flung flat by the wind-sucking hurricane blast of all the guns and lay on his back staring up into the brightening fresh day where the gunships in their squadrons pivoted, using the bodies of Bravo Company as their marker, and fired endless battering volleys into the Chuck regiment, The Bee wondering how many times a man had to die to be safely dead and out of that war. Then he knew. Just once.

Part II

6.

Zap

The Bee and Waldo stood in the trees watching the dustoff choppers swoop down behind the curtain of steel provided by the Crocodile gunships and incoming artillery to pluck away the bodies of Bravo Company. "How many Bravos survived?" asked Waldo.

"None," said The Bee. "Only the lieutenant. He was so big and heavy it took those three guys to carry Baddie, and they took his bullets for him. Bad's alive."

"In every horror there's got to be one to go home to tell the story. I suppose he's it."

"He is," said The Bee. "He'll tell it true."

"He can't tell it all," said Waldo. "He doesn't know it all. We got to make what's coming next."

Waldo looked away back to the south into the valley they had just left, toward where the ruins of the downed chopper lay, looking away from the racketing battle on the hillside where five battalions of paratroops were piling out of slicks behind their gunship protection and piling into the 95-Bravo Regiment of Chucks. It was going to be a very big fight here on Old Baldy. It was going to win for everyone everything they wanted.

Maybe even a front page article in The Washington Post to be passed from hand to hand in the Pentagon for a day or two. Maybe some happy stripes or a star or two. Maybe a medal from the hands of the President. Whatever it was, it would not be enough. Because what the Bravos had come here to do still had to be done.

Zap

Waldo adjusted his heavy load — the artillery net radio, Lieutenant Bad-Henry's M-16 with its precious Starlight scope, the M-79 he had taken from the dead grenadier, and his multiple bandoliers of ammo and grenades — and turned downhill toward the valley. "Let's go," he said to The Bee. "We've got a downed chopper and one M.I.A. to find."

The Bee adjusted his own misshapen pack of rats and ammo, threw the ute strap over his shoulder to hold the '16 at hip level, and stepped into the forest with Waldo. In minutes the clattering-KRUMPING screaming wailing battle on the hill was behind them and only the occasional ricochet sizzling through the treetops reminded them of it, and of the thirteen dead they had left on the slope, the twenty-six dead lying in their bunkers at their temporary base in the jungle, and Fruitcake, the country boy who wanted a medal, the first lost, on the civilized side of Old Baldy.

Zap

They tramped into a world where spirit and courage are not wasted. Through the green jungle canopy glittered diamonds of pale morning light. A tawny brushbuck bolted across their path. The first bird of the new day stretched yellow wings and leaped cawing between the branches into the sky. They humped along in their field stink, their ragged filthy bloody fatigues, their smeared and half-bearded faces. They had been leaned by steamy jungle marches and constant electric fear. Their minds had been honed to an unmovable singleness of purpose. They were traveling light. Pure soldiers now. The Department of Procurement's Vietnam War far behind them. V.C. Valley ahead.

Now it begins

It was at 0600 hours with the forest already hotting up that The Bee and Waldo, sticking under the canopy to avoid the trigger-happy air cav in their choppers and preferring to cut no trail but instead tramping an awkward route around trees and through brush, heard Fruitcake's trademark chicken cluck. He had never learned to whistle.

"That's Fruity, ain't it?" said The Bee aloud. "We're The Bee and Waldo. C'mon out."

Fruitcake unfolded his long body from the brush, a grin creasing his dirty, pimpled face. "Well, well, where you been? Didn't think I'd ever see you guys again, you got so damn lost."

"Took us a while to catch up," said Waldo. "What's our disposition?"

Fruitcake pulled off his bush hat and rubbed it over his sweating scalp. "Tell ya the truth, got myself a little bit separated from the company. Don't know where it is. Where you goin', Lieutenant?"

"South. There's an M.I.A. still out there, from the downed chopper."

"Is there?" said Fruitcake. He licked his lips and adjusted the '16 on its ute strap over his shoulder. "You're a little bit crazy, ya know? Two guys strollin' through Chuckie's Valley by theirselves."

"It's what we're doin'," said The Bee.

Fruitcake gazed off into the jungle. "Well, now. I got it in mind to catch up the company. I'm the best point man there is and they need me. I'll tag along with you two as we're all three headin' south, three guns better'n two." He smiled out of his grime. "Ya wouldn't have any C rats, would ya, you could spare? I could use some ammo, too."

Waldo pulled off a bandolier of ammunition and passed it over. "You figure three of us can put the fear of Uncle Sam into the 95-Bravo Chucks?"

89

"I figure we might try," said Fruitcake, wiping mud from the bandolier and looping it over his neck and shoulder. "They ain't really seen American soldiers before. They got 'em a surprise comin'. I'll take the point." He loped into the brush.

* * *

Twenty centuries east below the morning sun and away from that piece of jungle where three lone soldiers tramped lay the immense American basecamp outside the refugee hamlet of An Khe. Five thousand soldiers lived there, with beer, burgers, P.X. dollies, donut dollies, and plenty of fresh-mown grass for softball. Out of the basecamp and straddling its perimeter line of machinegun towers, stacks of concertina wire, landmines, and fifty-gallon oil drums rigged with explosive charges, stood Hong Kong Mountain, honeycombed with Chuck tunnels dug there when the French held a small fortress on the same site, where they built their pretty little lime green airport tower that now brought down on the Golf Course transports and choppers. The Yanks owned the basecamp, Chuck owned the mountain. Sometimes the Yanks would go up there and fight Chuck. Sometimes Chuck would come down off his mountain to blast away at the six basecamp 105mm howitzers manned by thirty gunbunnies who, because they were afraid of Chuck and had no confidence in the five thousand noncombat soldiers with whom they shared basecamp, had built their own barbwire, guntowered, mined perimeter within basecamp. But the peace of exhaustion, the peace of the five armies, prevented too much nastiness. Most afternoons, when the American clerks and the delighted-to-be-invited grunts who were R-and-R'ing in basecamp took out their bats and balls and made up their games, Chuckie would sit on his mountain eating his fish-reeking muck and cheer on the teams.

Tanks patrolled the dusty roads through the weeds. Mamas and Papas in their jeeps mounting .30 machineguns swung out through the tall weed looking for enemy infiltrators and Yankee deserters hiding in abandoned bunkers. Occasionally there would be a scare and a few companies of overweight clerks and cooks would be rousted out to sweep for landmines planted in the night. They would use their bayonets for that work, sticking them gently into the earth to feel for the metal, hoping there was nothing there to find. They were issued bayonets for this occasional work when the field grunts had to steal bayonets and whatever else they carried into combat. The clerks all packed their wicked-looking bayonets in their suit-cases and took them home for souvenirs.

Their nights were protected by startling bright lights from the gun-towers, by long racketing machinegun fire, and by the thumping and whooshing of the six basecamp howitzers. Each of the five thousand men in basecamp had a weapon of some sort issued in his name — usually the obsolete M-14 rifle with its .30 slugs. It was obsolete because it wasn't like the Flash Gordon little black plastic M-16 rifle, meaning it was heavy and old-fashioned and made of wood. But you could throw the '14 against a tree, drag its action through the mud, never clean it and it would still be loyal to you and save your life, more than could be said of the '16. It took a good soldier to make a good rifle of the M-16, a thoroughbred that needed lots of tender care, plenty of gun oil, lots of clean rag or she would forget to work just that one time you were staring brother Chuck in the face, him with his big heavy obsolete Nazi-invented, Russian-made, Chi-nese-copy AK-47 assault rifle that never jammed. Five thousand men and five thousand weapons, and on any night 4,950 of them felt naked and afraid. The last fifty were the grateful grunts just in from the field too drunk or too heavily asleep to give a damn what came down off that moun-tain at them.

Those 4,950 were afraid, so they dug down under the central mound of the camp and there built DeeTOC, the Division Tactical Operations Cen-ter. There was no division there anymore. That had been the First Air Cav, the cowboys who had cleaned out this territory and made it safe for Saigon democracy. Their work done, the division had gone north. They left behind their hole in the ground, the red leather chair for the Great White Father — the commanding general for this Area of Operations — and a bunch of Time magazine clippings proving how wonderful they were. No one made mention of the fact that the First Cav had lost its colors in Korea to those Chucks and for that shame the army would not allow it back into Burgerland until the Cav had redeemed itself in blood, or so the story went as told by ordinary grunts, who noticed that the Cav went at its redemption with a passion for news clips.

In that hole in the ground there was another hole, one filled with desks made from old ammo crates painted gray, a cot with a rubber air mattress, plastic-covered maps pasted on the walls and littered with grease-pencil marks, and a dozen squawking radios, and a junior lieutenant and a senior sergeant. They were the Fire Support Coordination Center, charged with keeping friendlies from killing friendlies. The lieutenant had a routine of twelve hours' duty and twelve hours in the whorehouses of Sin City, something else left behind by the Cav. The N.C.O. had a routine of twelve hours' duty and twelve hours at the gambling tables in the N.C.O. Club. They filled their spare time watching Combat! on television and playing checkers. The N.C.O. was Staff Sergeant Raiby, pale, crew-cut, lazy except at cards, thirty-two. The other was Second Lieutenant Engle, intensely bored, freckled, college dropout, buck-toothed.

"We're gettin' us some peculiar static out of the wrong place, Lieutenant," said Raiby, tuning the dial of one of their infantry net radios.

Engle set aside his copy of True Man magazine and perked up. Even nonsense was better than boredom. He listened, sighed, and said, "That static sounds like static to me."

"It's on the old Bravo Company freak, that's what it is," said Raiby, tuning closer.

They listened together.

Engle said, "Naw, just static. Probably all those choppers working out on the 95-Bravo Chucks are drifting over onto that freak."

Raiby shrugged, turned down the volume, and sat back, reaching for a mug of coffee, letting the static play itself out. They had a dozen radio nets to monitor — grunt, zoomie, paras, Crocodile, convoy, Hawkeye, armor — and there was always some weird static somewhere. Better static than another drunken Rock soldier getting on that net and singing "The

Eyes of Texas Are Upon You" in Korean as they liked to do just when the Great White Father had all his Batcos in DeeTOC for a pep talk. Raiby listened absently to the static. It seemed to have some form but unidentifiable. Maybe some element far down south, their trans just trickling up.

He looked across the radios into the bigger hole of which their Fire Support Coordination Center was just a part. No one else was listening for static. No one else cared. He looked up at the huge countdown clock no one ever used except to tell him when to go back to his bunk. It was too many hours before Raiby could leave to his card game. He looked at the starched-fatigue infantry officers with their bunker pallor, shoving breakfast burgers into their mouths as though they'd ever been out on patrol with no time to eat, and sneaking bourbon into their coffee.

Raiby drank coffee from his mug and thought about the three kids and wife at home, the kids pushing into the teens, costing him plenty. He had his nightly game and could count on another few hundred in money orders going through the army mails to his wife with each outgoing post. He was a good steady breadwinner. If he extended his tour in this bunker, pulling down Sergeant First Class or maybe even Master Sergeant – if he could go that high without going into the field – Raiby could go home satisfied he'd done his best by his family in the war. He listened a moment more to the peculiar static out of the Bravo freak, and then put it out of his mind.

* * *

The Bee tramped south through the Valley with Waldo and Fruitcake. The short-timer's calendar sketched in pen on his faded camouflage helmet cover — the helmet swinging from his rucksack — showed he had six months in the war, an old-timer. But six months on a Burgerland clock is twenty years' worth of campaigning in the jungle. He was an old man of eighteen. Haggard. The brightness in his eyes was not his fast-passing youth but alertness born of fear. He was exhausted from being spat upon by children, by jungle tribesmen, by whores. Exhausted from watching people forced to rummage through his garbage for food. From seeing

burnt-out homes, ruined fields, beer cans strewn everywhere. From counting the heaps of his mutilated enemies and of his mutilated buddies. He
was a dog that had been kicked too often. He craved love but knew he
was turning mean. Was he too far removed from the good man he had
been before the war ever to find his way back? If a man is to live among
his own kind he must cut his trail to things in life that should be important
to him — courage, love, friendship. But The Bee had no idea how to do
that. No one had shown him the trail before the war and now he was lost
in enemy territory. He was terrified of everything but mostly of himself.

A lifetime ago, The Bee had wangled a pass into An Khe to get out of
the field for a day's R-and-R and to be alone. He drank black market
Yankee beer bought from dusty roadside stalls, standing there in the heat
and steam along Highway 19 where it cut through the ramshackle refugee
hamlets. Wandered toward the brothels and steambaths of Sin City.
Looked in all the little roadside shop stalls as he walked. Spotted a haggard old seamstress in a new-made stall — she may have been twenty-five
for all he knew, Vietnamese women seemed to him to collapse from the
delicate charm of seventeen to disastrous old age at twenty-five. But how
much of that was the war? He looked in there to see a naked baby playing
under his grandmother's sewing machine. The seamstress looked up at
him and smiled. She was a new refugee in An Khe, she didn't yet hate
G.I.s. It was not the smile of a merchant, bartender or whore. It was an
ordinary smile, an everyday decent smile.

Bee stood in the hot sun and found himself smiling back at her, the first
time in centuries he had done anything with his face except eat, drink, and
gripe. He pulled off his bush hat and tromped into her shop. She seemed
so incredibly small and old to him. Her skin was burnt to coffee but shim-
mered with life. Her long black hair was bundled in back and her eyes
were of such a rich chocolate brown that he could not see the irises in
them.

He saw that she was suddenly frightened of this pale-faced, stooping,
smiling, Occidental giant, so he sat down on the matted floor. He picked

up the baby with a naturalness that surprised himself. It had been an immeasurable span of time since The Bee had wanted to hold a child. He held the baby an afternoon. At the end of the day he returned to the war. An old woman's smile and a naked baby made his single most vivid memory of Vietnam.

For Fruitcake in the lead of their little column, the war was a different matter. Like most soldiers he was a fatalist: Great uncomfortable events impinged on his life, things beyond his comprehension moved him where they would, it was all he could do to dodge among all those forces to keep himself alive and marching. A soldier in combat is a natural animal with no past or future and only two choices — fight or flee. Fruitcake knew that. Mother Army had taught him that good lesson, and in doing so had made him a coward. It happened when Bravo Company met Waldo for the first time.

Waldo was then attached to Charlie Company of the mech infantry as an artillery Forward Observer, drank nothing that wasn't vodka and drank that all the time, was a natural in directing steel and the F.O. every grunt company wanted because Waldo's companies came out of the boonies whole. He kept the enemy at arm's length, pounding him with steel, saving grunt lives. He did it all himself — unlike other F.O.s, he permitted himself no recon team – no recon sergeant, no radioman – but chaperoned his companies alone, doing everything himself, carrying that damn heavy Prick-ten radio with his fifty-pound ruck of rats and a little ammo for his .45. He wanted responsibility for no one but himself. He might sacrifice himself for his company but he would not risk a recon team.

The Bravos cheered to have Waldo come to them, but first they had to save Waldo from himself.

* * *

When the Bravos first met Waldo at dawn on that bloody, torn piece of Highway 19 called Bridge 25, he was on his way to L.B.J. – Long Binh

Jail. Waldo's own Batco was himself typing the stencil orders at that moment to send him to prison for cowardice and desertion in the face of the enemy and for refusing the legal order of a superior officer.

That had been the one-hundred-and-first day in Waldo's war. Autumn leaves, autumn grass, eternal summer sky. He had blown away ten million flowers that day with indiscriminate Harassment and interdiction Fire into the free-fire zone to keep Chuck off-balance. He was pulling the easy duty of temporary Executive Officer to the six-gun battery inside base-camp – inside its own fortified camp inside basecamp – while the regular X.O. took the cure for a busted leg. Waldo stretched along the warm sandbags of the main bunker, flexing arms and legs, dreaming of C rat pizza and watching a heli lift from the Golf Course, its defoliating guns retracted, enjoying the soft ease of basecamp life as the summer sky faded to an insect-chirping evening.

"Alpha Rear, firemission!" barked from the radio in the command shack.

Waldo and his bunnies ran to their stations as the jumble of words, names, numbers poured through the radio and the evening was begun, a long banging whistling evening supporting an infantry fight to the south, the howitzers banging out charge-7, the biggest load, making the hard-packed earth jump, raising thick clouds of dust and bitter blue cordite to fill the firebase. The man who did not keep his hands clapped to his ears would go deaf. Even at that each blast of the six guns was like being slugged by a heavyweight champ with a pillow around his fist. The guns slammed out their rounds in bright sparking flashes against the black night. Waldo imagined the snub-nosed shells arcing up over the refugee town, then falling down into the jungle far beyond An Khe's eastern border and bursting in whumps! of spreading steel.

He went from gun to gun as the firemissions ran, one mission blending into another, some guns firing one mission and some another. Waldo inspected the powder charges in each canister to make certain that each was correct and that the shells would be thrown far enough and high enough to strike on target, neither short nor long. His reeking, buffeting, throbbing night suddenly showed palest salmon at the horizon. He was astonished that ten hours of war had passed so quickly.

"Bring up the battery defense rounds," he called to the gun crews. "Use 'em up. They're getting old and stale."

A gunbunny dived into a bunker, glad to get away from the ear-splitting migraine-making slams of the howitzers, and began hauling up the rounds kept specially prepared for short-range defense of the guns. Waldo inspected each as it came out of the bunker.

He turned from his inspection of the canisters to watch the lay of the artillery flares he had been firing from the base piece for a different mission and turned back to see the gunbunnies pass an old round to a G.I. who rammed it into the breach of his howitzer — a round unchecked by Waldo – and the assistant gunner pulled the lanyard and the guncrew turned all eyes to their acting X.O. when the gun popped out the round at a charge-1. A pop! Not the deafening slam of charge-7.

Waldo, gagged with fright, smoke and cordite, jumped around to look toward the town expecting to see there an orange fan of bursting steel tearing apart houses and people. But he saw nothing! The round had cleared An Khe. Fallen on its far side. He grabbed his charts and plotted the trajectory for a charge-1. He measured the lay of the gun. He recalculated. The round should have cleared all the outer eastern shantytowns. He picked up the radio and called battalion Fire Direction Control, reporting his error. He continued to fire missions for troops beyond the town and others prowling the jungle. He nagged these troops, despite their running gunfights, for confirmation of a short round. None came. No reports of friendly casualties in the hamlets. No farmer reported a surprise short round. Where was that thing? What had it done? What had he done?

The guns banging over his head gave him a beating as bad as if he had been in a losing fistfight. The deep Asian night dragged on, the horizon that had once run salmon unwilling to welcome another day of combat with the thing in it that terrified Waldo. A dozen times he replotted the trajectory of the short round. He could not believe it had overshot the town. It might have gone into a house and been a dud and not exploded. Maybe that! But it would have gone through those poor wood and tin shacks like a tank. There would be dead. The firebase was fogged with smoke and dust and the taste of cordite. The heat of the guns roiled over him. He paced the firebase with his .45 in his hand, loaded and cocked.

"My God, Lieutenant, you've got to put that pistol away," said the Chief of Smoke.

"It was a short round, Smoke," said Waldo.

"No one reports a short round."

"Then it was a dud. There's a village there. It took out a hootch!"

"More likely you center-punched a water buffalo. You haven't hurt anyone. We'll check it out after dawn. Holster that pistol."

"I killed someone."

"This is war. People get killed. Why don't you put away that weapon until we see about things after light?"

"I'll keep it with me."

"So if we get a report you knocked down someone's hootch, what'll you do with that .45?"

Waldo went away into the smoke of the guns.

In the first of reddening dawn, Waldo abandoned his post and went looking for the short round. He walked alone through the wire and napalm mines around basecamp carrying only his pistol, cocked and ready for himself. He went alone through two villages east of An Khe, followed his plotted course across Highway 19 to a seamstress shop, through the silent crowd gathered there, into the shanty that no longer had a roof, into a room where he found an old woman and baby crushed beneath his fifty pound dud projectile.

The morning minesweep tank found Waldo alone walking west along Highway 19 toward the thousand French graves in chalky Mang Yang Pass, his helmet lost, his .45 in his hand dangling at his side, his eyes too wide and too bright. They took him on with them because it was still Chuck's country until the sun was fully over the horizon and the mine-sweep patrol had checked the road for boobytraps. They took him into the first fight of the day. Two B-40 rockets crisscrossed in front of the tank commander's nose and he fell back into his M-48 screaming but his driver had the presence of mind to turn the machine into the enemy rockets, showing the toughest of its shell, and the gunner fired one round beehive, the millions of tiny metal flechettes shrieking through the tall grass where the enemy lay. The tank took the third Chuck round neatly through its soft underbelly as it ground down off the road onto the shoulder, blowing fire through all its apertures and knocking Waldo from the tail where he had been clinging, the heavy dying tank grinding over the enemy bodies pierced through every square inch by the tiny arrows.

When the grunt Batco came down with his choppers after the fight was done and found Waldo there in torn fatigues, streaked with tank grease, bandoliers of rifle ammo across his chest, pistols under his web belt and a rifle in each hand and the chopper radio screaming that Strongpoint-7 was under attack, he took Waldo back up with him, shoving a grunt Prick-ten at him and shouting at him to put it on redleg freak and call fire for the Strongpoint, and Waldo did. The whole day went like that, choppering from fight to fight, Waldo calling fire, moving from unit to unit along the road, firing his rifles out of bunker loopholes, standing one-handed on the backs of racing tanks with his radio handset in the other hand clapped to his ear and mouth, scrambling into choppers and out of choppers. He fought every fight that day with every grunt unit on the road. He escorted both convoys of the day. He called Phantoms for bombing runs. He used Spooky's aerial gatlings. No one in his battalion knew who he was or where he was because he refused to use his call sign. A nameless voice came out of the battalion F.D.C. radio and the chart plotters knew that voice was the voice of battle and they went to work for it. He finished his day on Bridge 25.

Waldo sat with the security force holding the bridge, eating the rats they gave him, drinking from the canteen water they passed around. Because they knew his reputation, they found vodka for him. But he did not speak to them and they stopped trying to speak to him. Evening drew down. The last bright Lambretta three-wheeler full of chopped wood and the last Coke girl and the last bike boy scuttled across the bridge for the eleven kilometer rush back to An Khe and safety. Chuck prowled in the night and they were afraid of him, but worse were the American artillery and the helicopter gunships that used all the countryside as a free-fire zone after dark, churning up the earth with steel searching for Chuck.

Two tracks ground up onto the bridge, their weary troopers jumping down onto the asphalt for their chow. The bridge guards dragged the barb-wire barriers across the road at both ends, sealing the bridge. The guards went into their bunkers to do a little mild boozing and to listen to Hanoi Hannah. They had girls in there. It was midnight of the same night when the Hardluck Kid almost stepped into the main bunker as it took a B-40 round through eighteen inches of sandbagging and he staggered out covered with what looked like smashed tomatoes, wide-eyed and screaming. Again that nameless voice filtered into the stifling, dusty cramp of the battalion F.D.C. in basecamp, and the howitzers began firing.

At L.Z. Schueller, eight klicks east of Bridge 25, The Bee and Bravo Company were enjoying an evening's R-and-R out of the field, luxuriating in sleep in safe bunkers and eating good artillery chow, when the alert gong rang shrill and the bunnies ran for their guns, and the mech infantry-men clustering around their tracks began shouting, "The bridge! The bridge! Chuck is trying to blow the bridge!"

"Saddle up!" shouted the mech platoon leader, a lieutenant, his men already leaping atop their boxes, checking their weapons.

The artillery base commander ran out of his command post dragging on his shirt, saying, "Hey, hey! You can't go out there! We got standing orders not to let anyone outta this firebase after dark!"

"Chuckie rules the night, buddy," said the mech lieutenant, "but that's half my plat on that bridge – he don't take them without takin' me." The track lurched forward, the mech grunts leaning into the wind, the brims of their bush hats pushed flat against the crowns, hugging their rifles and holding onto the gunshields.

Another track rushed up, empty but for gunner and driver. "We could use some help," said the gunner to Bad-Henry. Ten from Bravo swarmed onto the track and it ran out onto the black road, oblivious to landmines, Chuck ambushes or the errors of the gunships swarming overhead. At eight klicks and around the leaping curves of hills and roadway, they could hear the larger bangs of the artillery crashing down and see the orange and green tracers arcing up from the bridge.

They roared down the road, two boxes, twenty men, all guns blazing into the night, and behind them — over the protests of the firebase commander — a Patton tank of the 69th Armored and one more track filled with Bravos came grumbling out of Schueller. They rode to the sound of the guns, like good cavalrymen, and they overran the bridge wire, firing and shouting into the black night, scoring on the users of the green tracers, and here found the bridge blown to bits, the bunkers torn down, pieces of bods scattered everywhere, the Hardluck Kid stained red standing in the middle of it all spraying fire down into the small stream bank, where Chucks screamed and flung satchels up on the bridge around him. They grabbed the kid off just before the asphalt was blown from a charge set beneath the bridge and the bridge ruptured, and it was then, there, in that, that the army taught Fruitcake the soldier's code. He was trembling and drooling with fright, his M-16 and all his bandoliers empty, the bridge blowing up in his face, and he saw Waldo stagger out of a bunker that had just fallen in. The first relief tracks were stuffed with wounded and the track commander had flung his big box around and was ready to race back to Schueller, his own men peppered with bullets and two of them down in the track well sprawled on the ammo crates bleeding to death, the blazing dragon's roar of the approaching tank and track flashing at them from the darkness of the road east, the Chucks pouring in clever and heavy fire, and no one but Fruitcake saw Waldo there. Fruitcake leaped off the track before it sped away and dragged Waldo out of the dust. "Great God!" Fruitcake cried. "We're the only ones left alive on the bridge!"

The first pair of relief tracks had disappeared into the night, guns empty of ammo, and the tank and third track with the Bravos had not yet roared down to them, and there they were, stretched out on the fractured asphalt, no cover, Chuck bullets like a steel wall above them, satchels exploding around them. It was then Fruitcake determined never again to be in a fight. To keep away from the main body of men that must always suffer and die. To always take for himself the safety of the point man. He knew himself for a coward and he was satisfied with the knowledge because it would keep him alive.

He dragged barely conscious Waldo into a heap of ruptured sandbags and stuffed him down there among them, building a tomb of bags over him to protect him. He scrabbled along the bridge grabbing up dropped rifles, loose mags, stray cartridges, hand grenades, and flares and crawled back to Waldo's makeshift bunker and crawled in with him. The Chucks swarmed up onto the ruined bridge as he knew they would. Just before the tank arrived they would swarm away. In that interim of thirty seconds they would kill him and Waldo if they could, they would rob all the bods, and they would turn Yankee weapons on the Yankee soldiers when the tank arrived.

Fruitcake opened fire, and when he did, he drew fire from the enemy, a shattering screeching gut-turning, sandbag-bursting fire. The coward wept with terror as he fired back. He scrambled from ruined emplacement to ruined emplacement, hurling grenades and drawing fire away from Waldo lying stunned among the sandbags. The Chucks were swarming over the bridge, running at him in loincloths, bodies greased, bandoliers of AK-47 ammo crisscrossing their chests, some with satchel charges slung at their sides. They were firing from the hip as they ran toward him, so confident, and surrounding him.

Suddenly the .50 fire from the tank's big machinegun exploded on the asphalt of the bridge – it exploded there! – and the Chucks were leaping off the bridge into the water. Fruitcake with his long spider legs ran back to Waldo, all his ammo spent, all his grenades gone, only his bayonet in his hand, and then the tank was there beside him, G.I.s scrambling off its tail to grab him and Waldo and stretch them down on the tank's tail for safety. More G.I.s leaping off spraying fire. The big tank gun blasting huge gouts of yellow over their heads. G.I.s searched the bridge for the wounded and the dead, and then they were gone back into Chuck's night, steaming for Schueller, the gunships orbiting above the road pouring red streams into the riverbed. Waldo had come conscious and was crouching there, one hand clinging to the back of the tank turret, the other on the tank's radio handset, groggy but calling fire on the bridge, fused to burst overhead and scatter bits of slashing steel all over the bridge without harming the valuable road.

In less than fifteen minutes they were back at the firebase and saw that they had stormed out of the place without waiting for the barbwire barricades to be dragged back, the barricades were crushed. Fruitcake and Waldo dropped down from the tank.

Captain Foley, Sar'n Mars, and Lieutenant Henry Bad-Henry stood there. "Give Waldo a drink," Bad-Henry said to Mars. The first of morning split the sky, they glanced up at it surprised. Waldo wiped from his lips the plastic staleness of the bourbon from Mars's canteen.

Foley looked at Waldo like a child who's just gotten the Christmas toy he always wanted. Bravo could use a good F.O. It could use any F.O. The last one was dead. "We ain't got one. You unattached now, Lieutenant?" said Foley.

For Waldo those words were like being welcomed back into the human race, forgiveness after killing an innocent old woman and infant, after killing a man swimming away his lazy afternoon, after everything else. Here with the Bravos he could be his own man, the lord of fire of a dense and furious land with the power to save lives in exchange for the lives he had taken. Sometimes things can be that simple. Sometimes they can be that awful.

Fruitcake turned away from Waldo. The battle that had revealed Fruitcake's cowardice he could see in Waldo's face as the beginning of Waldo's self-redemption. Fruitcake hated battle. He knew he would turn and run if he could. But the bridge fight proved he had imprinted on his soul the soldier's code, something he had never known he had learned. Despite his slinking cowardice, that damnable code would not let him abandon his company. He was one of them. They depended on him and he on them. He was a coward who could not be a coward.

As for Waldo, what he did to welcome the morning made him a Grunt For Life with Bravo Company. He picked up a radio and called into his battalion, using his proper call sign, to report where he was. His battalion commander got on line, raving with fury: "Get your ass in here!" the Batco shouted, "I got a slot reserved for your ass in L.B.J.! You abandoned your post in wartime! Over, you bastard!"

"That's right," said Waldo. "Tell the X.O. with the leg he can have his six guns back. I'm humping out with the Bravos, over."

"Listen, you damned coward, this is a direct order — get your tail in here, over."

"I had enough, Six. I had enough. I had damnhell enough. I'm humping out and that's all I'm going to do. Your M.P.s can come find me in the Valley. Send them for me there. Out."

Waldo went out with the Bravos and stayed with them. It was Bravo's battalion commander Colonel Yoden who saved him from L.B.J. Good F.O.s were few and too easily killed – because they were overworked, spent too much time in combat – for Bravo Company to give up any F.O. it could beg, borrow, steal or kidnap, especially one with Waldo's reputation for bringing his grunts back alive. The artillery Batco tore up the stencil he had been typing and mused, with Yoden, that, after all, Waldo and Bravo Company might just pull down a couple of Silver Stars for their colonels, especially if there was some way to infiltrate them into the Valley where they could stir up a very nice little fight with Chuck. "We gotta look at things in the long term," said Yoden. "We take a little lip, let those guys get their blood up for it, and they'll do us some good fighting down in the Valley."

"Yeah," said the artillery colonel. "Then we get us some stars where it counts — on the shoulder, not the chest."

The stencil with its prison sentence drifted into the trash can. The two colonels began to plan some war for Waldo and those stupid grunts out in the boonies.

7.

At midmorning with the sun well up and their fatigues stained black with sweat, Fruitcake stopped just shy of a Chuck trail and signaled for Waldo and The Bee to squat in the brush. They went down smoothly to one knee, weapons ready, the brush around them not moving and their clothing not scraping it. They squatted alert and unmoving for many minutes, their eyes moving in slow sweeps through the jungle, cutting it into sections, peering through the gentle breeze-drawn tug of leaves and the skittering motion of lizards on tree trunks, looking for that larger irregular motion that marked the movement of men.

Fruitcake loped uptrail, measuring the width of the enemy trail, looking for cast-off bits of equipment, torn fragments of cloth, and finding, instead, the marks still wet where men had stepped out of the column to urinate against trees. This was Chuck's valley and he moved boldly here, in big units carrying heavy packs and big weapons. He was not afraid here. Fruitcake squatted by the trail, listening into the south, and was satisfied that, despite the fresh urine marks, the column had moved quickly and was now far away. He slid back to the others. "How many you figure?" asked The Bee.

"Thirty-fifty movin' fast," said Fruitcake. "From some blazes on tree branches, I'd say they've got them some 82s with them."

"Movin' south," said The Bee.

"Company must be down that way," said Fruitcake. "They're going after Bravo."

"We'll keep moving south ourselves," Waldo said, "but we'll cut trail from here at right angles to this one, swing out west and then drop down. Wherever Bravo may be, we know that the guy from the downed chopper is down there and we want to get to him before the Chucks do." He tuned his radio to the Bravo freak and spoke softly into it, trying to raise the company. "No go," he said at last. "Battery's weak or the mountains here won't let us commo." He tuned to the grunt battalion headquarters frequency and reported the enemy trail and direction but there was no reply. "We'll move out on skirmish line," said Waldo. "No machete work. Backtrack if we must but we leave no trail."

They moved out abreast, five meters between, each virtually lost to the others save for an alert hand signal, a cluck or the sight of a black plastic rifle in the jungle greenery. They went due west, stepping over the enemy trail without disturbing its marks, and leaving no boobytraps to raise questions in Chuck minds. They marched through the heat of the day when the birds, lizards, insects drowse in their treetops and the snakes crawl away into the mushy earth. They came to the edge of that piece of forest and drew back from the bright sunlight beyond. They chose a hard bit of ground with stones and fallen logs for a rest stop. Two drowsed against their packs while one watched. They ate what little they had that could be eaten without the noisy work of a P-36 can opener. They lay motionless an hour and then were gone, slipped into the brush, their eyes sweeping the jungle ahead of them looking for the telltale marks of a man's passing or of a Chuck ambush waiting. In late afternoon birds and insects came alive with fury, birds *cawing* across the treetops, mosquitoes buzzing after them. The mosquitoes had their fill, none of the three would risk a slap or smear on the mosquito repellent Chuck could smell.

In late afternoon, now moving south following the jungle toward the downed chopper, they again found the trail of the Chuck column, the urine marks hot, the mushy earth of the fresh-made trail beginning to fill with water, and the jungle creatures just beginning to crawl out of the holes into which they had fled in alarm at the tramp of so many human feet. "Figure we're ten minutes behind 'em," said Waldo quietly. "Trail's moving out southeast now." He sketched the enemy route on his plastic map – Chuck was marching south but keeping well within the natural S-curve of the forest as it grew south from Old Baldy into the valley. Chuck was afraid of the gunships working out on the south side of Baldy and wanted to attract no attention down here.

The Bee measured with a finger the depth of a sandal print on the soft Chuck trail. He said softly, "I can't figure it. Why is this unit marchin' south, away from the fight up there? They ain't carryin' no wounded. These're all fresh men, heavy armed."

"It's the company," said Fruitcake. "They're goin' after Bravo."

Waldo folded away the map. Cupping his hands around the handset and lying prone on the soft earth while the others searched the forest with their eyes, he called the grunt battalion to report the change in direction of the trail.

* * *

Staff Sergeant Raiby, paler from even more days in the command bunker buried under the only hill in basecamp, took the hamburger the buck-toothed and very-bored-with-the-war Second Lieutenant Engle handed him and shoved half of it into his mouth as he put his ear to his radio monitoring the grunt net. His eyes ran over the cards he had laid out practicing poker hands. He wiped ketchup from his lips with his hand and said to Engle, "We got any Lurps down south in the Valley, Lieutenant?"

Engle, chomping his own burger, mouth bulging, shook his head. "Nope. Why?"

"Damned if there ain't some commo coming out of the Valley."

"It's that business on Old Baldy, Sarge."

"Don't think so. This is the second trans to blueleg higher. First was garbled and weak. This was good and clear. Somebody down there calling himself 'Yonkers two-four' reports a high-speed trail and thirty Chucks moving southeast."

Engle stopped chewing. "Can't be. Yonkers two-four is Waldo Whatshisname and he's dead. Where's Meese? Hey, Captain Meese!" A thin infantry staff officer with an eighteen month bunker pallor looked up from his comic book. "We got anything at all down south in the Valley? Lurps, Beanies, anybody?"

"Naw. Everything's up on Baldy."

"Well, Cap," said Raiby, "we got us an errant trans here, and it's a little weird."

The captain continued reading his comic book as he crossed the concrete bunker floor. He looked up from the magazine and said, "Yeah? What ya got?"

"Sarge here thinks he's got Yonkers two-four on the grunt net," said Engle.

"Imposs," said Meese. He thought about it. "Yeah, well, never got his bod back, you know. Waldo, I mean. But those things get blown apart sometimes and there's nothing to get back. That's two-four, right?"

"You think he could be out there two klicks farther south? We just monitored a report to your higher of a Chuck trail leading southeast."

"Naw. We couldn't account for one of ours, too – The Bee. When you don't extract them the first time, you don't get them at all. Tigers eat them. Chuck eats them. What kinda trans was it — dustoff?"

"Just the report of a Chuck trail."

"I ought to be getting that report from higher in due course," said the captain, returning to his comic book. "But I'll check with them now and see what they say. It's just a freak freak coming off Baldy, that's all."

* * *

Waldo, Fruitcake, and The Bee stepped across the enemy trail and shrank away into the brush, dropping down to the earth in slow motion, their eyes searching the jungle to the limits the jungle permitted. There they squatted, barely within visual contact of each other, for many minutes. The trail was too fresh for chance-taking. If Chuck thought he was followed, he would leave a bushwhacker behind him. More minutes passed. Jungle creatures frightened into their holes by the passing Chucks crawled out. The G.I.s slid away, disturbing little of the brush, avoiding the rasp of leaf on cloth, moving in a skirmish line.

They humped like that through the late afternoon making another five hundred meters through moderate brush and heavy canopy. As the first of dusk began gathering among the trees, they heard the snap of an enemy bipod connecting with an AK-47 barrel and they went to ground, sliding down to the damp earth like men being drained away into the mud. They waited, forcing breath to come softly and silently. When there was no more sound, they waited longer. At length, they heard the chunk of an entrenching tool digging into earth, a man's laugh, a few words in rapid-fire Vietnamese, and caught the whiff of a small cook fire and roasting meat.

Waldo motioned to the east. They slipped separately into the brush and moved slowly around the enemy base, drawing back farther into the trees when the noise of work or the rattle of metal indicated a machinegun position. They continued eastward until far from the sounds of the camp being dug in, until dusk had filled the spaces between the trees with haze and the heat of the day had changed into a warm, mild evening, the sweat drying on their faces and backs. As evening quiet drew on, they drew together in the thin shelter of brush beneath a thick stand of trees.

"What do you think?" whispered Fruitcake. "Should we call fire on 'em?"

"Ain't no doubt they're Chucks," The Bee said softly. He rubbed a hand over his sun-freckled forehead, bursting dozens of tiny blisters, wiping their water on his fatigues.

"Yeah, we're going to do that," said Waldo. "What say I put a range and def spread on 'em and when I do we run southeast?"

"Might find that a problem," said The Bee. He removed his hand from the earth to show the tiger track into which he had put his hand. Eight inches across.

"That's a monster," said Fruitcake.

"She's movin' southeast, where we wanna be."

"Everything's moving south," said Waldo. "Everything's going after the downed chopper."

"The Chucks back there, they got a little different idea from us, though," said The Bee. "I think they have it in mind to set up a bushwhack at the downed chopper and blow away anyone who comes down the valley on foot or in gunnies to extract that M.I.A."

"Yeah, they'd do that, the bastards," said Fruitcake. "It'd also draw the paratroops south and take pressure off the 95-Bravo Chucks on Old Baldy."

"That wouldn't be too good for our side," said The Bee. "The Chucks can cut Bravo's trail and know that Bravo is searching for the M.I.A. but the Bravos won't know the Chucks are comin' down on 'em."

Fruitcake rubbed his inflamed mosquito wounds. "We gotta get south and find the company, that's all."

"Night in an hour," said Waldo, looking through the breaks in the overhead canopy. The birds had begun to settle into the treetops, chattering their evening greetings, nestling down for the night ahead. "All right. We call fire."

"Good!" whispered Fruitcake.

"We try again to raise the company by radio, too," said The Bee.

"Right. Then we run like hell southeast, we skirt the Chucks, and once we're in thick brush we sleep in the trees. Keep away from that tiger. First light, we move out again following the forest line south or southwest and we search for the chopper and for Bravo, whichever comes first. Right?" said Waldo.

"It's a plan," said Fruitcake.

Waldo raised the handset to his mouth, stretched out on the ground, and spoke quietly, calling for Bravo Company. No answer. He switched to the artillery frequency and called his battalion F.D.C., gave his fire commands, and waited for confirmation.

* * *

"Lieutenant!" said a radioman in F.D.C., looking astonished at the radio that had just crackled with Waldo's fire commands. "What do ya make of that?" He had the nasal tone of a repaired harelip.

The Fire Direction Officer had stopped in raising the bottle of Coke to his sun-peeling lips. He put down the bottle, motioned toward a computer, and said to the soldier, "Plot it."

"There, Lieutenant. Two-klicks-three south of Baldy, so it ain't nothin' to do with the paratroops," said the computer, setting aside his compass and ruler.

"What the hell could that be?" said the lieutenant. To the radioman, he said, "Answer him. Tell him to I.D. himself properly."

The R.T.O. with the harelip spoke into his mike and Waldo replied, his voice crackling out of the radio's loudspeaker: "This is Yonkers two-four and this is a firemission, over." His voice was distant, thin, whispered, broken with static.

"Can't be," said the lieutenant. "Waldo's missing and that means dead." He sat in the oppressive dank of the bunker sloshing the Coca-Cola in its bottle, staring at the F.D.C. radio until it said, "Yonkers one-eight, this two-four, do you hear me, over."

"Tell him we hear him," said the lieutenant. The R.T.O. did. "Tell him to sit tight for five secs." The R.T.O. did.

The lieutenant cranked up the field telephone and put the handset to his ear. "Let me talk to Six," he said, his battalion commander. "Six, this is one-eight. Got a strange trans from two-point-three klicks south of Baldy. Someone calling himself 'Yonkers two-four' wants a range and def on a V.C. company. Right, he said 'two-four'...No way to confirm, and we can't get a chopper down that way. They're all up on Baldy and you know those chopper boys — they won't leave a fight when they've the upper hand...Shall I fire it? Roger." He put down the field phone. "Tell two-four or whoever it is that we're going to drop a range and def spread on his target."

The computer gaped at the lieutenant. "You mean Six actually thinks it's Waldo out there?"

"No. But Six won't take any chances. Maybe there's a lost Lurp team down there. Besides, a target is a target. We're here to kill targets."

"Or some Chuck with Waldo's code books and his radio," said the computer grimly as he leaned over his plotting board, wiping sweat from his face, working his compass and ruler.

"Shoot it anyways," said the lieutenant. "Then we'll send choppers down when we got some free and see what it's all about." The computers bent to their work at the plotting board, moving rapidly, and the R.T.O. began to call fire commands to the guns at L.Z. Action in the west in the maw of the Mang Yang before battalion F.D.C. turned over the mission to Action's F.D.C.

The R.T.O. called Waldo: "Two-four, this one-eight, we have your range and def coming in thirty secs, over."

"Roger," said Waldo. "We're moving out, out."

* * *

Waldo, The Bee and Fruitcake slipped away into the brush, moving quickly now to get far from the target area and stray rounds. They wanted to be a thousand meters distant but they were barely two hundred when the whistling overhead brought down the first artillery rounds and they went to ground, groveling in the soft earth, praying that that one-in-a-thousand short round didn't find them in their little piece of jungle.

* * *

"Call the Crocodiles," said the lieutenant to the radioman. "Give 'em that logger. Tell them we want a sniffer down there right after dark. We want to see if we killed anything more than a few thousand monkeys. Then we want to see if a sniffership can smell whoever the hell that is calling himself 'Waldo.'" He stared at the marks on the plotting board. "If he is alive, what's he doing that far down in the Valley?"

"If that's Waldo, he's exactly two-point-three klicks farther south than the last part of Bravo was when it walked into the 95-Bravo Chucks," said the computer, tapping his grease pencil on the charts.

"What's he doin' down there?" said the R.T.O.

"Whadya mean, 'he'?" said the computer. "That ain't Waldo. It's somebody else."

The R.T.O. with the harelip turned to the computer. "You just plot 'em, my boy, but I listen to 'em. I know every F.O. in this territory by voice inflection and commo style. I'll reenlist if that ain't Waldo."

The computer blinked sweat from his eyes. "Then tell me, wise ass, why the bastard didn't run north like any sane man would instead of running south into that stinking Valley?"

"He's down there, I don't know why. He's down there and he's killing Chucks like he's supposed to do."

"You're both nuts," said the lieutenant. "Waldo's dead. I liked him and I wish he wasn't, but he is. Let's shoot this and then we'll go see who's using his call sign."

* * *

At that moment, in DeeTOC under its mound in the center of basecamp and three hundred meters from the redleg F.D.C. bunker, Sergeant Raiby glanced at the countdown clock and saw that he had barely another hour more duty before he could retire to the N.C.O. Club and his cards and a bleeding steak. He stretched back in his warp-legged metal chair and did a doodle on the action roster where he and Lieutenant Engle had kept track of all the action in the Area of Operations for the last twelve hours. It had been more than a busy day: Bravo Company had been wiped out, with two missing and presumed tiger meat, and only one survivor — their Executive Officer, the ex-ballplayer who'd never pitch again thanks to his arms and legs being shot full of holes and one nasty AK-47 round somewhere in his lungs, First Lieutenant Bad-Henry, now in a Qui Nhon hospital looking out on the white beaches and the Korean surfer girls, the lucky dog.

Waldo's voice came thinly through the redleg net to artillery battalion F.D.C. and Raiby froze. "Engle!" he shouted across the bunker. The lieutenant looked up in exasperation from his checkers game with Captain Meese – it was the first time Raiby hadn't prefaced Engle's name with his rank. "Come listen to this! It's Bravo company again!" Every head in the bunker turned. Here was something to kill the boredom.

Staff officers crowded Raiby's radios. The thin voice whispered from out in the jungle somewhere within earshot of the enemy, broken with static from a weak battery or no altitude for the antenna, speaking in the silent bunker with its fluorescent lights and its starched fatigue staff officers. "He's using the Bravo F.O.'s call sign," an officer said, "what is this?" They listened through the wait as the redleg F.D.C. paused, evaluating what it was hearing, and they stared at each other in disbelief as the F.D.C. announced it would fire the mission.

"They can't shoot that," said Engle. "There's nobody down there. This is a false trans. It's a Chuck with Waldo's radio."

Raiby crowded the radio speakers. "Been gettin' lots of strange static out of the Bravo net," he said. He fine-tuned the radio to Bravo frequency. "Nothing now." He sat back in his metal chair, staring at the radio on which someone calling himself Yonkers two-four had just spoken. He listened to the empty static and so did the officers, until they got bored, rubbed their clean-shaven chins or scratched their trimmed scalps and went back to their desks, keeping the countdown clock in view waiting for their shifts to end.

Engle, still leaning over the back of Raiby's chair, said, "What do you think, Sarge?"

"I think somebody's down there."

"Smack in the wrong place to be. That's Chuckie's Valley and once the fight on Baldy is over, every Chuck in the world is going to be streaming down there on top of him."

"Yeah, it's weird. A soldier in the wrong place at the wrong time, and he's trying to fight his own war all by himself."

* * *

Over the crash and tear of the arty rounds gouging up the forest, Waldo, The Bee, and Fruitcake could hear one clear rising scream, unchanged by the blasts of steel, climbing to that awful shrill like metal being torn. Then the range and deflection spread — a battery of six guns firing together over a checkerboard five hundred meters on a side, firing one column of squares at a time starting at the center and working out, then in, then out — moved on and the screaming stopped abruptly, leaving a hollow in the roar of the exploding metal. A vast silence gripped the jungle. The attack was finished. No more sounds from the enemy position.

The three G.I.s got on their feet and moved quickly to the southeast as full night fell. They stalked through brush to a cluster of thick-trunked trees, ambushed the trees and the forest ahead for a long hour, the howls of wounded and dying Chucks coming to them only faintly and occasionally through the brush, blackness filling every part of the jungle and the night animals crawling out around them. They were too far from the ruined enemy base to know what was happening there, and they didn't want to know.

One by one, the other two guarding, they climbed up into the trees, each man in his own tree, putting themselves up far enough to be safe from tigers and deep enough in treetop foliage to avoid being spotted by Chuck Starlight scopes. They used their utility straps and pack straps to tie themselves in their trees, slinging their rifles from their necks, bracing themselves on heavy limbs, rubbing mud from their fatigues on their faces and hands for camouflage. They ate quickly and quietly, listening deep

into the jungle between chews, and fell into the sleep of the forest animals
– a wakeful, watchful sleep.

They woke together or in turns as night lizards skittered across
branches, as owls hooted away from them in surprise to find them up there,
as one lone cat — only the deep sound of its rasping breath identifiable to
them from the dank blackness below them — prowled toward the ruined
Chuck camp, as the yowls like babies' cries of other tigers echoed over
the forest. Night insects bit at them, snakes passed them in the leaves, a
startled tarantula dropped from The Bee's pack to the ground.

Overhead a heli clattered, a slick with two doorgunners and a second
slick for shotgun. The sniffership was fitted with methane breathers, the
human body gives off methane. It was searching for proof there were bods
down there in that charnel house of jungle the artillery had made of
Chuck's base, and also searching for proof that the radio trans that brought
on the devastation was made by a living, breathing Yank F.O. named
Waldo, out there in the jungle all by himself. The sniffership clattered up
into the black sky and went home. It had found proof that the artillery
expenditure had not been wasted. But it had not sniffed Waldo's scent
through the thick forest canopy.

The men in the treetops drowsed again. Late in the night, two great
cats spat at one another, then shrieked in mutual outrage, waking all three
soldiers, and they knew that the man-eaters had found the Chuck camp.
They slept. A single silent orange round, a ricochet, streaked up over the
trees toward the waning moon. It woke all three of them. They knew then
that Bravo Company, or some part of it, was truly down there south in the
Valley. They slept again, without snores, without movement, without
dreams, the sleep of the forest.

* * *

At 0400 the night had already proved a brilliant success for Staff Sergeant Raiby. At long last he had been promoted into the high stakes game
in a back room of the N.C.O. Club, a game for senior master sergeants,

majors, and one hotshot second looey from the Twenty-fifth Infantry Lurps – the crazy Long Range Patrollers – who insisted on coming to each game with his shoulder holster over his camouflage fatigues. The majors, wary of the Lurp reputation, made him hand over to them his pistol's magazine. The Lurp lieutenant sat there smilingly boyishly around his stogie and raking in the winnings in chips, U.S. Green, and the Fu Manchu local stuff.

That night, his first in the big time, Raiby got the Lurp lieutenant's goat. Raiby began raking it in around 0200 and kept at it until 0400, when the Lurp threw down his cards, spat out his stogie, begged the pardons of all the majors present, and stalked out of the N.C.O. Club, his pistol's magazine in his hand. Raiby had pulled in fifteen-hundred dollars in those two hours. He could have done more but he was a shrewd and careful gambler who knew the limits of his luck. For him, gambling was like playing the stock market, an investment to make money for his family's future. He played, too, because he loved the game, the challenge, the threat. But he always quit ahead because he wanted this war to see him home in triumph, his bank accounts bulging.

It was a very French night in the highlands, he thought, cool and thick, full of mist, with fog up on Hong Kong Mountain sprawling out of base-camp, the beacons of the radio relay station atop the mountain peering dismally down on the camp behind its barbwire and guntowers. An occasional fine rain swept across the fields and Raiby stood in it feeling the cold tingling on his face, clearing his head of too much cigar smoke, beer, and hard concentration at five-card stud. It was a night for strange notions. That old mountain, the ancient village beyond the camp barricades, these wild roads and jungles and battered native people, the haunting memory of the French legionnaires who had once stood on this same piece of earth, and of their thousand graves on the west side of the Mang Yang. Standing there he could believe in eternity because it seemed to be all around him in the changeless earth and this endless war, in which he had a small part, small and safe enough to suit him.

117

The six-gun battery in basecamp, barricaded behind its own loops of concertina wire, began to fire, their reports coming muffled — *poof-BANG!* — through the mist. Another man came out of the club, his head snapping around first to the sound of the guns, so Raiby knew him to be an artilleryman. The man unzipped his fly and urinated on the ground, saying to Raiby, whom he did not know, "I like this kinda night." He had the nasal tone of a repaired harelip.

"Me, too," said Raiby. "I can sleep and there're no Chucks likely to come down off Hong Kong."

The man zipped up. "Night like this makes you wonder about things. Ya can't explain everything that happens in life, can ya?"

"Least of all here."

"Ya heard about Bravo Company?"

Raiby waited to hear what the man would say.

"Well, I'm down there with the redleg, ya know, in the batt's F.D.C. bunker. I'm the R.T.O. I know *all* our F.O.s by their voices. I should — I've listened to 'em all plenty." The man gazed up at the beacons peering down on the camp from the mountaintop.

"So?" asked Raiby uneasily.

"So I got a trans from one of our F.O.s who's dead."

Raiby looked around at the man. "Who's that?"

"Waldo. With Bravo. They're all dead and he's missin' and presumed."

"What's your batt gonna do about it?"

The man shrugged. "We fired the mish he called for and in the A.M. we're sendin' out a chopper to look-see. No one really believes it's Waldo. 'Course, none of 'em in F.D.C. or battalion headquarters have listened to Waldo over the radio as much as I have."

"You think it's him out there?"

"Sure it's him."

Raiby stared off over the perimeter as it came alive with the racketing of orange machinegun fire. Another crazy Lurp tower guard was relieving his boredom. "Pardon me, I got me some work to do." Raiby trudged up the DeeTOC hill and went into the bunker, the night shift surprised to see him. He stayed there the rest of the night, listening to the radios he fine-tuned to the redleg and the old Bravo freaks, drowsing sometimes and listening rapt other times as strange throbbing unidentifiable static crack-led over the freaks.

Engle came in at 0600 on schedule and cried, "You take this damn war too damn serious, Sarge."

"Could be," said Raiby, putting his ear to the radio speaker to listen to the Bravo freak. "Could be I do, after all."

8.

Well before dawn the good soldiers of three units had rejoined the war. Waldo, Fruitcake, and The Bee had awakened and hung unmoving in their treetops until the first of predawn had barely colored the edges of the sky above the trees and issued a vaguely paler shade of night into the forest beneath them. In laborious and patient silence, moving with skill and grace, they slipped from the treetops, taking many minutes to bring themselves to the ground, choosing the places to put their feet long before they touched earth – like spacemen uncertain of alien soil – and then drifting away into the brush to squat and watch dawn come over the forest. This was the dangerous time, the worst part of a soldier's day, when ambush cost lives.

They shrank back into the brush, wordlessly patrolling a circle of forest ten meters across until they were satisfied it was momentarily secure. With their hands, two guarding, each scooped a small hole to defecate, burying it with his hands. They moved away from there toward the southeast — toward where that orange American tracer had rocketed during the night — on skirmish line, pausing at the moment the sun finally came fully over the horizon and into the trees. They shrank into the leaves, taking five minutes to open a can of food each and to eat and then bury the empty

tins and again wordlessly, using a minimum of hand signs, moving southeast after that startling moment of full flashing jungle dawn had passed.

* * *

As this happened, a second element of Chucks, another group of forty
whose trail Waldo and the others had not crossed, edged out of their anx-
ious forest hideout into the artillery-ruined Chuck forward operations base
on which Waldo had called fire last night. They found thirty-six men –
eighteen killed, ten wounded requiring hospitalization. It is far better to
wound a man seriously than to kill him — a wounded man needs a lot of
valuable resources to save his life and is a burden and hazard to his buddies who must see him to safety. Eight only who had survived, buried
under heaps of dirt thrown up by the incoming batteries of artillery, the
earth saving them from the flying chunks of steel that tore to bits their
comrades.

The second Chuck element knew it had only the time between false
dawn and true dawn to recon the wrecked base and to evacuate the
wounded, that American choppers would be there with the first full light
to gloat over the dead. They swept across the base astounded at the
churned-up, hopeless horror they saw – what the arty had not destroyed,
the big cats had. They withdrew into the jungle with the ten wounded and
the eight whole and the pieces of their dead. What could have brought on
such destruction? This was no blind shot, no harassment and interdiction
fire. They had seen or heard no helis overhead except the one that had
come over after the attack to sniff the dying. Nor had they crossed the
trail of any Yank unit this far south – Americans went in big groups with
a lot of equipment and left big obvious trails. Their prey — Bravo Company, operating strangely alone and circled up in its base in the forest
clearing — was too far south to have detected the unit here and to have
called in the hand of the destroying artillery.

No, they realized as they sped away from the ruin, searching the forest
floor for signs, there was something else down here, another unit too small

to detect easily, fast-moving, clever, something as strange as Yankee guerillas. It must be the Lurps, the second element decided. Until they came upon the marks where Waldo, Fruitcake and The Bee had crouched beneath a stand of trees when Waldo had called fire on the Chuck base. Three men! Just three? The Chucks were astonished. Not even the Long Range Patrollers, all wild men, went in units of three. For the Lurps, five was a minimum and they preferred ten. For the short-range ambush patrol teams, fourteen at minimum, with three M.G.s and enough other weapons, grenades, mines to arm a Chuck company. Three men alone in Chuck's private valley? Absurd. But there it was, plain to see in the faint impressions in the soft jungle floor. Three men.

They worked quickly to bury the eighteen dead, or the parts of them that were recoverable. They did that to deny their enemies the advantage of knowing just how many the artillery had killed. With the first churning of air overhead by the American choppers and the first flash of true dawn, they slipped away with the wounded into denser forest to work their way west into the folded hills matted with brush and trees, well protected by heavy weapons and spider holes and a few antiaircraft machineguns, to the underground field hospital of the N.V.A. Yellow Division. Twenty men were sent on this duty with their leader's report of what had happened, and the unbelievable account of the three Yankee guerillas operating independently in Chuck's private domain.

The remaining twenty marched behind their young and now very curious captain, a man named Dong whose cheeks had been crushed by the concussion of a Yankee Phantom's bomb, his face scarred and smeared by that bomb and his ears melted and glued to the sides of his head. The weeks of shrieking pain that wound had caused him did not keep him out of a war where a professional of his caliber in a bitter war of attrition was too valuable to retire. That and his curiosity kept him in the war. The Yanks fascinated him: What was the perversity in them that brought them 15,000 kilometers to fight a tiny war in a tiny country? Dong wanted to explain it. As for the war, Dong hated it. He hated the highlands, too. He craved his wife's fat body in the steamy south and he craved his old profession as enforcer for a minor lord.

Dong led the remaining half of his company in a slow and careful sweep of the forest, keeping away from the ruined base and the hovering choppers, to search for the three men who had brought on this disaster.

* * *

In the moments before false dawn the chopper pilots at the great American basecamp climbed into their machines and cranked on their engines, giving them the full thirty minutes warm-up the metal needed and so rarely got. At false dawn, arty and grunt observers piled into the slicks and they rose into the cold morning sky, drifting west toward the Valley following the gray snake of Highway 19 below. With full dawn, the slicks and a heavy escort of gunships from the Crocodiles climbed for altitude and hacked south, keeping well east of the forces on the south of Old Baldy blazing away at each other in their morning fury.

The choppers found the Chuck base buried under heaps of torn up trees and soggy earth. They hovered long enough for all the observers to manufacture a good body count estimate — there were no whole corpses but plenty of pieces, plenty of blood, and they mistook the marks where bodies had been dragged into the forest by tigers as the escapes of wounded men — and then they rose into the yellowing sky, each of them wondering who it was lost in this valley who had called the fire, and called it right.

* * *

Three G.I.s tramped through another hot day, skulking behind the thin protection of leaves to save them from the thing a soldier fears more than death – that screaming piece of flung-out steel crashing through the skull that leaves a man to die in hours of suffocating in his own brains and blood and terror or, worse, leaves him to live a vegetable life in some Veterans Administration hospital, poked, prodded, pitied. They moved with care and skill. Chuck's bullets had long ago taught them to be good woodsmen, something they had not learned on the marching fields of their Burgerland training posts.

The army had all the right ideas about this war, it just didn't believe in applying them. American soldiers were trained as guerillas but never allowed to be guerillas. The army taught them to be independent in combat, to move quickly, to make careful, well-aimed rifle fire, to use their initiative. But when the army put its well-trained soldiers into combat, it wanted them to stick together, to move on command, to spray the jungle with machinegun-like rifle fire, and to do nothing that would upset the plans of higher, plans designed to get higher medaled and promoted and home unscathed. The army didn't trust its soldiers.

No one but the combat soldiers thought of the war as a total war in which tactics and strategy *had* to work. Because the lives of the combat soldiers were held in forfeit. Only the combat soldiers, away from army constraints, fought the war the way it was meant to be fought — the way Chuck had determined it must be fought. Now three American guerillas tramped across the Valley's floor, and Chuck did not like their eerie change of character.

* * *

After a twenty minute rest break for chow and guarded nap, Waldo and the others pushed on. They came upon another trail, much lighter than the trail they had found the day before. This was the trail of a smaller unit. They crouched by the trail — it had not been cut through the forest but the unit had moved slithering around trees and obstacles, backtracking when it had to — and searched the forest with sweeps of their eyes, not moving their bodies for long minutes. At last The Bee crawled to the trail to check it out. He found one print of a boot heel. "It's Yanks, that's sure," he said.

"Chucks with U.S. boots on?" asked Fruitcake.

"Could be. But Chuck don't move that carefully in his own valley. It was a G.I. element. I think it was part of Bravo. Try the radio again," said The Bee.

Waldo did, no response. He said, "They may not have a radio with them or it could be knocked out."

The Bee wiped blister sweat from his forehead. "What do ya wanna do?"

"Skirmish line again," said Waldo. "Fruity, you take the right flank and keep contact with the trail. The Bee and I'll keep each other and you in sight. You lead us downtrail until the trail looks fresh, then we break off and move forward and hope to hell we can I.D. ourselves before Bravo blasts us."

"It's a plan," said Fruitcake. "Not a very good plan but all we got."

They moved out.

* * *

A kilometer behind them in the jungle the twenty Chucks led by the curious and melted-face Captain Dong also had come across the American trail and were surprised for the second time that morning. They had not expected any enemy units this far south. Now they discovered two tiny units moving further south toward the downed chopper through territory that, were the situations reversed, no Chuck in his right mind would traverse except at night in a heavy column well strung out for protection against Yank mortars and artillery.

* * *

When fear is constant, a soldier can then say he was afraid at a certain moment and mean that against the ground base of fright he was especially terrified. Except for first dawn, a soldier is only afraid in that way when he is approaching his own lines and his buddies don't know he's out there. That supreme terror was what Waldo and the others felt at the moment

Fruitcake, with the sense of danger only a self-admitted coward can have, signaled them to sink into the brush. Mid-afternoon, the sun burning through the thick canopy, their uniforms drenched with sweat. They took time to crawl together, moving quietly, making no leaf tremble, gathering together.

"The unit we're followin' is up there," whispered Fruitcake. "I can *feel* 'em."

They lay still, listening. Nothing.

"No one but an Indian could be that quiet," said The Bee. "They know we're back here and they're waitin' on us."

"They think we're Chuck," whispered Fruitcake, his voice trembling.

"They don't respond to radio contact," Waldo said. "We got to move up on 'em."

Fruitcake wiped from his brow the salt sweat that could blind him. "I'll push ahead. I'm the point man and I got a feel for just where they are. Wait here for my signal."

Waldo and The Bee stretched out prone – any bullets Fruitcake might attract, they didn't want to share. Fruitcake crawled forward slowly, slithering around branches that could give him away in movement, pausing for long minutes to catch his breath and listen ahead into the forest. He had low crawled twenty meters, his '16 dragged by his side, when he heard the slight scratch of a man shifting position on damp earth. He paused. No more sound. All right, he thought, this is it: "Fruitcake!" he cried, neither shouting it nor saying it too quick.

No sound ahead of him. Even the rasping of the jungle crickets disappeared.

He said it again, this time stretching it out: "Froootcaake! This is Fruitcake here, Bravo! Talk to me!"

Still no reply. This is really it! "All right, you bastards, Fruitcake is gettin' to his feet. He's movin' slow and easy with his hands in the air. Don't shoot. This is Fruitcake here." He got slowly to his knees, raising his hands with his rifle over his head, and looked down into the gray eyes of Corporal Pinball looking back at him over the sights of his shotgun. "Pinball! This is old Fruity here. Ya ain't gonna shoot me, are ya?"

Pinball jerked his head. "C'mon in, Fruity, quit shouting." He lowered the shotgun, keeping it trained in Fruitcake's general direction.

"I got The Bee and Waldo with me. They're back in the jungle a ways."

"Tell 'em to come in, too. But not to be too quick."

The country boy gave his chicken clucking signal, slowly lowering his arms and shifting his rifle to the crook of his arm, standing elaborately casual there to prove to Pinball – the only one of the American patrol he could see — that he wasn't the front for a Chuck attack. There were enough traitors in that war for that not to be an unreasonable fear.

Waldo and The Bee got carefully to their feet and came through the brush toward Fruitcake, leaving no tracks but making some noise so the patrol would know where they were and that they were coming in.

Pinball laughed softly, put down his shotgun, and stepped out of the shrubbery, grabbing Fruitcake, Waldo, and The Bee in turn, saying quietly, "Ya bastards! We never thought to see any of you again. C'mon in!" He led into a heap of brush in which Mars and the red-haired medic Specialist Fifth Class Cobb squatted with a ruined radio.

"Yeah, now I see why we couldn't raise you guys by radio," said Waldo.

"Well, the damned thing's okay, really, it just looks shot-up," said the medic. "But the battery took a round and spilled its juice. We did a little transmitting last night trying to raise the company and got back scratch."

"My radio's not much better," said Waldo. "Battery's about shot. How many guys you got here?" Waldo gazed around the forest floor. Some patches of fatigue were apparent here and there among the bushes.

"Thirteen including me, Lieutenant," said Mars. "I got 'em all spread out in a circle, within fingertip touch of each other, Nung-style."

"One good mortar round would take you all," The Bee said.

"Like they could get a round through that double canopy overhead," said Mars. "Anyway, this was temp. We got the feeling an hour ago we was bein' followed. We settled in here to see who it was. Glad it was you guys." Mars used a filthy army green handkerchief to wipe salt sweat from his dirty bald scalp.

"There's plenty of movement in this valley today," said Fruitcake. "Lots of Chuck. He could surprise us too soon."

"We got ourselves a little bit separated from the company yesterday," said Mars. "I think the company is just about due south of us now. At least that's our route unless you guys have a better idea."

"None," said Waldo. "If we push south, we'll find the company and the downed chopper's M.I.A., and that's what counts."

"Glad to hear there's one down there," said Mars.

"You see the fireworks last night?" asked Pinball.

"We caused some of it," said Fruitcake. "Waldo called fire on a Chuck company in the woods."

"Yeah, we heard that, too. We also heard south of us, and that's why we figure Bravo is down there — somebody had a sweet little fight with Chuckie about 0300."

Waldo said, "Okay, we been at this laager jabbering too long already. Let's move out."

Mars gave a low whistle and a few heads moved to peer at him through the brush. "We got Waldo back," he said, "and Bee and Fruitcake. We're goin' south after the company. Saddle up, move out."

This lost fragment of Bravo Company got to its feet and moved in two staggered skirmish lines through the jungle.

* * *

Behind them, Captain Dong paused in his pursuit down the faint trail left by Mars's little patrol and thought about the evidence he had. A small patrol, about the size of a Short Range Ambush Patrol, was moving south. It had picked up a three-man detachment. Sixteen to seventeen, maybe eighteen, men total. Too many for Dong's twenty man half-company to engage, especially since they were moving with a strange care and style he had not witnessed before in Yankee soldiers.

He shrank off-trail with his troops and pressed his radio handset to his mouth, calling his higher, checking on the locations of other Chuck and N.V.A. units in the Valley. He put down the handset. Every Chuck unit was up on the mountain the Yanks called Old Baldy, fighting the paratroops. There was precious little left down here in the Valley. But higher was sending a company south, heavily armed, to follow the American patrol's trail. That meant the captain's support would catch up in about four hours, dusk maybe. A dangerous time for units to meet but a good time to recon the enemy ahead and to decide what to do with the night. If the Yanks didn't find Dong first and call more of that artillery on him.

He glanced up at the thick overhead canopy. That could hold out most mortar shells but not a hundred-pound artillery shell. He gave the handset to his radioman. They crept south.

* * *

The Deerslayer — he had once mistaken a brushbuck for a Chuck on an ambush patrol — advanced through the woods with his M-16 in one hand and his blued bowie knife in the other and, just before dusk, found the ruins of last night's Bravo Company base. The rest of Sergeant Mars's patrol peeked at the remnants and drew back into the forest. Waldo came to the tree-line with Pinball. They studied the remains in long, careful sweeps of eye. "Damn thing is probably boobytrapped," said Waldo.

"I don't see anything that looks unusual there," said Pinball. "They had a fight last night but they kept company integrity. Then they shoved out south this morning and pushed in their bunkers. You can see they were pushed in and not rocketed."

"No sense in going out there to nose around," said The Bee. "Chuck has had this base all to himself all day. What I can't figure is if the company fought here last night, why did Chuck just let 'em walk out this A.M.?"

"Yeah," said Pinball. "And where's Chuckie now?"

"Down there," said Waldo, pointing south. "Between us and Bravo."

"What say we sweep around this F.O.B. and try to pick up the company's trail? Or the Chucks?" asked The Bee. "Then we keep off those trails though we keep 'em in sight as we move south?"

"Roger. That's what we'll do," Waldo said. "But we need some concentrated firepower ready right now just in case we find us a bushwhacker close by. We move out in column of twos if the trees permit. We keep quiet. We don't start any fights."

They swept around the abandoned Bravo base and found the forest deserted. At the southeast corner they found the marks where Bravo had penetrated the forest at first light. There they found the forest floor lacquered with blood turned black on the soggy earth, the brush, the trunks of trees. Bravo had circled up and driven off the enemy and then charged through whatever containment circle the enemy had thrown around the base, pushed through into the trees, and gone south. It had been a fast, bold, shocking maneuver, and it had worked. The trees for thirty meters into the forest were chopped and nicked from Bravo's running gunfight.

Deerslayer, red with mud, bowie knife in hand, came up to Waldo and The Bee and said, "I been over the ground, both sides, and count no more'n thirty Chucks here last night."

"That's not enough," said Waldo, surprised. "Chuck wouldn't attack a company of Bravo's size — that's thirty-three men — with just thirty of their own. Who would?"

"That's what they did. Musta figured they'd hold Bravo here until they got reinforcements."

"This valley can supply Chucks like it's got a production line for 'em," said The Bee, uneasy.

"Yeah. We got to assume not only Chucks between us and Bravo but they spotted either your trail or the three of us," said Waldo. "Time to start thinking the enemy is on our trail right now."

"'Slayer," said Mars, "I want you on our far right flank. You keep in contact with Bravo's trail and keep us goin' the right way. The rest of us will move out in two skirmish lines, staggered, and we'll follow your lead, got it?"

Deerslayer slid his knife into the scabbard under his fatigue jacket to keep it dry and went down the trail's shoulder into the brush. The rest of the patrol followed, spreading out quietly, moving quickly, M-16s, M-79s, automatic shotguns at the ready. They humped into the darkening dusk of early evening and still Bravo's trail did not warm up. They weren't going to catch up to the company before nightfall and they could not risk walking over Bravo's perimeter in the dark when their own buddies would shoot them for Chucks. Waldo called the halt. They shrank under the leaves. "Eat 'em cold," he whispered. "No smokes. No talk."

"No digging in, either," said Mars. "Makes too much noise."

Waldo said to Mars and The Bee, "When we got plenty of dusk, we get up on Bravo's trail and hump south fast. We put two point men out front and some flank guards. When we got plenty of evening around us, meaning you can just see your hand in front of your face, we pull off-trail and ambush it."

"Jesus!" said The Bee. "We only got the one machinegun and just two claymores. We ambush with that?"

"We do the best we can," said Waldo. "If somebody's following us or Bravo's trail, we'll blast them and run due east and set up Nung-style. Blast them once, they won't follow us again tonight. That'll give us a breather when we move out at dawn tomorrow."

* * *

Behind them, Captain Dong and his half-company approached the ruins of Bravo's F.O.B. of the night before as heavy dusk settled around the torn earth. He knew the base had been booby-trapped — that was standard practice for both Yanks and Chucks — and kept away from it, circling around the perimeter as had Waldo with Mars's patrol, checking for signs of what had happened and why. He found enough evidence to show that a Yankee patrol had moved off on Bravo Company's trail and then had disappeared into the forest, whether east or west he could not tell in the gathering gloom. That was something he didn't like either — the Yanks usually set up elaborate night camps, the kind of camps the Chucks would set up only in their Valley. This Yank patrol was full of guerillas, and there is nothing a guerilla such as Dong likes fighting less than another guerilla.

Dong squatted in the blood-stained earth at the entrance Bravo had made into the forest and decided that the Americans, unlike the Chucks, wouldn't move at night. They were no good at it. So the Yanks would be settled in somewhere as usual, wasting the night, while Dong's half-company would march. If he could push his unit another two hours, settle in and throw out listening posts, he might be able to catch up to the American patrol early the next day, look it over, and decide what to do about it.

But he had two more worries: The company of reinforcements coming fast down the trail behind him had not yet caught up. What if it came humping into him at night and his troops opened fire on it or the company's noise gave away Dong's position? Then the murderous Yank artillery fire would rain down on them as it had poured down on that unfortunate V.C. company the night before. Second, what became of the V.C. that had fought Bravo here last night? The marks showed that the unit was following the American company, but that it had been cut by a third — perhaps twenty men remained. If *that* unit was out there in the night, what would happen if Dong's half-company bumped into it?

Grim thoughts, all. He liked none of them. But he would not waste the night. He had to make time over the patrol he was following. But he would be cautious. Dong moved his men south rapidly, following Bravo's trail.

* * *

Mars organized the ambush. He preferred the traditional L-type to the fancier Nung mercenary or U.S. Marine things that only work if the men in them have been trained together in long hours of drill to do just that one

133

thing. Even though the L-type required three machine guns and they had only one. He put that one at the corner of the L facing uptrail toward the north. The short bend of the L ran perpendicular from the Bravo trail and had four men in it, all facing toward last night's Bravo F.O.B. and whatever might be following. The long arm of the L was laid parallel with the trail and about five meters from it in the forest among enough trees to give them overhead cover from mortars and some protection from enemy small arms fire, but with plenty of clear fields of fire to pour steel into the kill zone on the trail itself.

The long leg had nine men in it, including the machinegunner and his assistant gunner. Waldo, Mars, and The Bee took up their own positions: Mars at the far end of the long arm of the L to better keep fire control of his men, The Bee on the left side of the machinegun on the small arm of the ambush near the trail where he could look uptrail and down to watch for the approaching enemy, and Waldo snuggled down prone under his camouflaged poncho liner, his M-16 on its bipod in front of him, the M-79 he had scrounged from the dead grenadier two nights before by his side.

Although an L-type bushwhacker may seem to be off balance with all its emphasis on its own kill zone and no defense to the rear, the point of an ambush is surprise. If the enemy approaches from the wrong direction, the ambush lets him pass without molestation, provided he doesn't notice the ambush. Once an ambush is blown and the kill zone full of corpses, the ambush team grabs its equipment and runs, keeping what little ammo remains for a last-ditch defensive circle battle, if it comes to that. It rarely does.

The patrol was exhausted. None of them had much sleep in the last forty-eight hours. They had patrolled nonstop, kept alert through Chuckie's long night, and had little to eat. Waldo had them sleep two-in-three, huddling beneath their poncho liners and looking like mounds of earth among the trees. What was left of the moon rose and faded away. Waldo was careful with his use of Bad-Henry's Starlight scope mounted on his '16, knowing it put a glitter in the scope of any enemy Starlighter.

They slept in their turns the heavy unmoving dreamless sleep of the exhausted.

The point man of Dong's unit came up the trail, was up and past The Bee before The Bee overcame his start and nudged the sleeping man next to him. The nudge was passed down the legs of the L and the men, who had slept propped up on elbows behind their weapons, put their fingers over triggers or palmed claymore mine firing pins. Those who had grenades clutched them in both hands ready to pull pins and throw. Grenades would be useless to them in thick jungle but ideal on that little scratch of trail.

The Bee gazed uptrail and breathed, "Jee-zuz!" The trail, straight for ten meters there, was black from side to side with men. Two squads, he calculated. One squad more than a fifteen-man ambush team could be expected to attack. He gave the sign to the man next to him to do nothing, and the sign was passed on. The G.I.s, unmoving in sleep and barely moving in preparation for attack, lay still as Dong's half-company streamed past them down the trail.

Waldo waited a half hour, until he concluded Dong's the only enemy element moving on this trail, then passed the signal for the men to gather their gear and push off for the defensive fighting site they had chosen on the map, to the east. They went less soundlessly than in daylight but they went without disturbing the night birds or the sleeping monkeys. They slinked away from the Bravo trail and met together in a broad circle in the forest beneath heavy canopy that would protect them from mortars. They went to ground, lying on their bellies behind their weapons, those men who had claymores setting them out the required distance. Then they stretched out their arms and slid back into the circle until each man could touch the fingertips of the men adjacent. They lay like that through the night, every other man sleeping, his buddies on each side waking him when their turns came.

They expected an uneventful night. The only Chucks they had anticipated were Dong's and those Chucks had passed them without notice. But in the deepest of the night, at that moment when even the big cats fear to prowl for the absolute unearthly depth of the jungle night, something was moving and it woke them all. They lay rigidly alert, breathing softly, forcing themselves to keep it regular and quiet, lying there behind their weapons. It was Chuck.

* * *

The reinforcement company following after Captain Dong. It assumed that Dong's troops had cleared the way for it and moved quickly. After all, there had been no sound of Dong attacking the enemy or being attacked, so the route must be clear. This unit moved with skill through the night jungle, following a route parallel to Bravo's trail but well within the forest to avoid any sniffer helis and not to risk accidentally bumping into Dong's outfit.

Finally, the reinforcement company found a safe place to overnight. Its men drew up together and sprawled out tired on the ground as their leader used his radio to speak softly to Dong. This leader was a veteran captain of the 95-Bravo Viet Cong Regiment who had taken the political name Nguyen — as common in Vietnam as Smith in Burgerland. He had political ambitions, brave ambitions for a Northerner hated for being a double-minority — he was a Catholic and his great-grandmother had been Chinese. He had compensated for that prejudice by moving to southern Vietnam where to be Catholic was normal and where the hated Chinese were far away. Now he was surprised to find that Dong, a veteran blessed cursed with six years more experience in this valley than Nguyen, had moved so far south so fast without trouble.

Nguyen was determined to close with Dong as much as he could before giving his men a few hours' sleep. It would need both of their understrength units to sweep the jungle for the remnants of the company that Bravo had cut up the night before in order for them gather the strength to attack Bravo. He gave the order, his men came to their feet and tramped south.

* * *

They were skillful night marchers but they made some noise. Their truck tire sandals betrayed them as true Chucks and not N.V.A. regulars as they marched through Waldo and Mars's patrol spread out on the forest floor. None of the G.I.s moved as the V.C. stepped on the stocks of American rifles and kicked past American ribs, forty Chucks putting their feet on American hands as the Yanks prayed, the forest gloom so thick and the American camouflage of cloth, dirt, and shrub so complete that all forty of them marched through the American patrol without realizing they had penetrated one of the units they had come to destroy. The reinforcements trailed on south while the G.I.s gasped at their good fortune.

The G.I.s stayed prone and barely breathing the remainder of the night. None could sleep despite their exhaustion. The baby cries of the jungle cats filled their ears.

9.

At 0600 Lieutenant Engle came clattering down the angled concrete steps into the DeeTOC bunker and into the blue-haze of the fluorescent lights, leaving the brightening morning outside. He had been in the war for five boring months and he had not yet seen full daylight. "Sergeant Raiby!" he exclaimed, stopping flat-footed and staring across the banks of radios at his N.C.O. sitting there on his metal chair, eyes red-rimmed and face ashen with exhaustion, an ear cocked to the grunt net. "You pullin' twenty-four hour duty to show me up?"

Raiby glanced up from his concentration, irritated to be disturbed. "I can't get this Bravo thing out of my mind."

Engle clomped around to his favorite metal chair with a padded donut on the seat for his hemorrhoids. He threw down another stack of *True Man* magazines, his supplies for the day's twelve hours of duty. "How long you been here?" He glanced over the night log, saw that nothing special had happened — a few sniffer readings, Spooky worked out on Old Baldy to support the paras, another attack on Bridge 25 near Old Baldy – probably to try to draw Yank forces off the mountain and back onto the highway where Chuck thought they belonged – and a few small arms rounds taken on the basecamp perimeter from the village of An Khe, or more probably from Sin City where the girls entertaining the Chucks had over-beered them.

Raiby rubbed his stubble. "I been here since 0300, I believe. Might I borrow that razor of yours, Lieutenant?"

"Take it. You don't want the Batco trompin' in here seein' you in a combat shave. He'll start gettin' ideas about where you'd better fit in his organization. Like out in the field with the crawly things." He looked at Raiby in puzzlement. "Hey, if you were here at 0300 last night, what happened to your poker game?"

"I skipped it."

"Never heard of you skippin' a game. What's got you so bugged about this Bravo thing, anyways?"

Raiby stretched his shoulders stiff from hours hunched near the radios, listening to the grunt freak searching for a dead company and then the redleg freak searching for Waldo, who had been with them when they all died. Raiby glanced at the younger man – a few years younger, yes, but the kid had been to college and that seemed to make him younger still. "I'll tell you. It's something my dad said to me when I first enlisted. It's from the Old Army and they taught it to him in the Big War. He said, 'Never stop anything you start and never start anything you must stop.' I think I finally understand what the old man was saying," said Raiby. "I got this feeling that Bravo Company out there has the Old Army in it."

"Bravo's blown away. There is no Bravo."

"I know that. I do. Maybe I'm just so tired of this war and bored with whatever this is here I think up weird stuff to keep my mind churning over."

"That's what I'm beginning to think, too. When's your R-and-R?"

"Two months. I'm going to meet the wife in Honolulu." Static crackled out of the Bravo net and Raiby hunched closer to the squawker.

"Yeah," said Engle, watching him, "I think you need it, bad."

"Hey, look at this, Engle," said Captain Meese crossing the concrete floor. "Raiby, you, too, since you got it in your head that Bravo is still out there in the boonies." He flung a map on their desk, small red dots marked on it in grease pencil. "This is what Snoopy sniffed out last night. Look at it — almost three klicks south of where they should be, there was a bunch of Chucks in the forest, three groups of 'em, and be damned if they aren't moving off south, away from the fight on Baldy. What the hell for?"

* * *

The second morning after Bravo's disaster on the south slope of Old Baldy, the patrol with Waldo and Mars in command and Fruitcake in the lead stirred to their crouch in the moments before false dawn. The forest was asleep and silent. They crouched unmoving during the seeping in of dawn among the trees, watching around them with sweeps of eyes. Then they pushed south, quietly, and went to ground again at the moment that true dawn flashed through the trees. They secured an area along the sandal-printed path of the Chuck forty-man company that had walked through their ambush in the night, breakfasted lightly and quickly, took their turns in the brush, watched for a while, and then pushed off south again, keeping each flank on the Chuck company's trail and the Bravo trail where Captain Dong with his twenty men had gone.

* * *

Below them in the valley, Dong's half-company and Captain Nguyen with his full-strength company finally linked up, amazed that neither of them had found the Yank patrol nor any sign of it. The realization struck them: They must have tramped past the patrol in the dark. They had walked through an American ambush — replete with enough firepower to stock a Chuck company — and the Yanks had not fired. What kind of Yank unit was that? Farther south, they could hear the faint echoes of battle. Light machine guns and automatic rifles, a few grenades. The unit down south that had caught and fought with Bravo Company was mixing with Bravo again, a thing it should not do until it had been reinforced by the sixty men of the two captains' units. But what if Bravo Company had set a trap for the remnants of that company down there? A company-sized trap? Were the damned Yanks trying to out-Chuck the Chucks? Preposterous. But what was going on in this Valley that Chuck owned?

Nguyen's company moved south toward the distant firing, knowing they would not arrive in time to help but only in time to pick up the wounded. Behind them, Dong spread his half-company across the forest and followed at a slower pace, a powerful rearguard to screen against the sudden descent of Waldo's patrol. It would do no good to be caught between two American elements, especially when they acted as strangely as these acted.

* * *

Farther north, the American patrol began to move away from its breakfast rest stop. Fruitcake took the point. Deerslayer and a grenadier with good eyes took the flanks. They moved in a column, rapidly, ready to bring heavy fire to bear should they walk into a trap. There were too many Chucks in this piece of woods to move on skirmish line. They marched through the morning, while Waldo used his radio sparingly to try to raise Bravo Company far south of them. He failed. Here, among these trees and hills stretching to the mountains that shaped V.C. Valley, communication even with the powerful receivers back in basecamp where the artillery F.D.C. waited for their call was impossible. Waldo got nothing but static. Of course, it also meant the Chucks in this part of the Valley were likewise deaf, and that was good. Waldo listened for any choppers overhead or aircraft to whose freaks he might switch to use them for relays to basecamp, but there was none. What was the point of sending anything flying this far south into the Valley? It was Chuck's valley and no Yank should be down here.

They marched slithering around brush, using no machetes, leaving the barest trail, seasoned soldiers in enemy country, weapons ready. There is only one useful thing about close-order drill and parade ground marches

– they make a soldier feel like a soldier. Now these soldiers tramped in their sweaty torn dirty fatigues, their makeshift equipment and packs slung on their shoulders patched and torn, the fighting weapons in their hands grimy and specked with rust because they'd not had time to clean them properly, but as they tramped they felt like soldiers on parade. There is nothing so grand as being in the middle of a body of men in uniform and parading in blocks of units across a flat grass field beneath your guidons and flags and a pure blue sky, your rifles and bayonets flashing: You feel part of something powerful, and indeed you are. You feel that you can tramp through vast desolations and terrors to the edge of the Earth and back so long as those flags flutter and the cadence count rings true. They marched feeling that way into the depths of the Valley, feeling grand, powerful, unbeatable. Nothing could turn them back, they were sure: They were the grand Chuck-killing Army of the Republic.

They moved under lighter canopy where the forest had thinned and a man could see twenty feet instead of just five, where the forest floor was crawling with grab-your-ankle vines, wait-a-minutes, come-alongs, and the birds in the treetops, unalarmed by the quietly passing patrol, chittered at them glad for the company. The two Chuck units ahead had made no effort during the night to leave no trail, they were easy to follow. At high noon the patrol came upon the place where the two units had joined, paused for breakfast – leaving their own tins and wrappers in the brush, carelessly hidden – and moved south. Waldo's patrol had not heard the gunfire from Bravo's morning fight but it was obvious now that the combined Chuck force ahead of them was going down after Bravo Company. But again the Chucks, too confident in their own territory, had left plenty of signs of their intentions: The main body had gone south rapidly in column while a smaller group had spread out to march south more slowly, screening the main column's rear from whatever might come down the valley. Odd that Chuckie was being so cautious in his own valley. That could only mean he thought something was following him, that Waldo, Mars, Fruitcake, The Bee and the others were on his trail. They started off southward into the forest and knew that they could not go in there carelessly. A Chuck element was there as a rearguard and may have set up a bushwhacker. At the least the Chucks would have planted mines.

Waldo, Mars, and The Bee crouched under the brush as the patrol spread out around them and sank down out of sight. Waldo unfolded his plastic map. "We get into some rough country ahead. Hills, folded ground. Good place for Chuck to ambush. We want to try to flank 'em before we get there. Look at this — we got this little mountain here to the southeast. Plenty of tree cover over the crest —"

"Says the map," said The Bee.

"That's all we got to go on," said Mars. "Seems to me these Chucks are stickin' to the valley because they expect Bravo to stick to the valley, like we always do. Let's go up this mountain and down, march fast, and put us ahead of Chuck or on his flank. Either's good."

"Yeah," The Bee said. "Could also dump us smack between two Chuck elements."

"It can do that."

"I don't see any other choice," said Waldo. "I don't want to walk through the forest after Chuckie has had time in there to set mines. We'll cut trail away from Chuck right now and go over the mountain."

Fruitcake led out with Deerslayer as the right flank guard to report when they had finally broken contact with the Chuck trail. The trail curved south-southwest. They moved quickly, worrying less about making sound or leaving tracks, but avoiding machete work — machetes ring like good new bells.

The mountain was 180 meters high, barely a foothill anywhere else in the world. Its lower half was thick with new-growth trees all rising up straight and true, with little underbrush. It was easy climbing, full of switchbacks. Fruitcake found the fastest paths. The heat of the day became intense but they were in the cool of the trees. They found a swift-running little stream of crisp cold water, drank their fill, and rested under the trees by the stream. Some men lolled back against their packs to drowse while others sat quietly staring into the forest, their eyes that had been strained from watching so many days and nights now cooled and refreshed with splashes of stream water. Mosquitoes buzzed, fire ants tramped in columns across the trail.

"Let's go," said Waldo.

They got their feet and climbed higher. They came to the military crest of the mountain after just two hours' labor and found that, despite the map's promise, it was barren but for waist-high elephant grass. The American maps were thirty years old, modeled on poorly drawn French charts. "We move east," Waldo said. "We keep in the tree-line and we got east around this crest, then down the south slope." They headed east, moving swiftly now, abandoning the effort to make no noise or leave no trail because this unplanned extra piece of march was going to cost them too much time. They did not want to spend another night out of Bravo's protecting perimeter.

They found the eastern slope even more barren than the crest: The mountain slid away to the east and southeast through thick elephant grass and boulders, and beyond its slope lay a panorama of all of Vietnam — the rugged wrinkled mountains leading to the haze of An Khe on the horizon, beyond that the sparkle of light from the glass windows of vehicles zipping through the American basecamp sixteen klicks distant, and the pale blue bowl of sky overhead. The land was yellow, green, brown, cut with snaking blue-black rivers, filled with slapping-bright, insect-buzzing jungle reeking of rotten nuts and animal droppings and infiltrated by yellow vipers, and by forests like back home, forests with needle-strewn floors, tall, straight brown tree trunks, and birds chirping from the limbs. They went quickly around the mountain into the open, quietly, with apprehension: Chuck could see them too easily, but they had to risk it to make time.

The slope was far steeper then they had expected. Fruitcake cut a narrow trail barely a foot wide and they moved along that, the steep slope of the mountain breaking away beneath them. They moved crouched against the face of the slope, grabbing bits of grass or plant roots to hold themselves to the mountain's face, their heavy packs and weapons threatening to drag them down into a boulder-bouncing roll into the fields below.

They plunged into young forest on the south side with relief, breathing heavily not from exertion but from fright. They regrouped and moved downslope, angling to the southwest now, and came across the second branch of the little stream they had crossed coming up. Here the stream burst from the mountainside in many places but had not run in volume to make a clear flow. Here it drained downslope in a long, curving alley of mud. The soldiers, footsore and hungry for rest, jumped onto the mudslide and slid down the mountain, following the stream's curves around trees and roots and boulders, lying back on their packs to slow themselves and stretching out their legs for speed, slipping down in silent, wordless, child-ish glee.

The mudslide dropped them near the valley floor in a place where the draining water had encouraged a marsh, elephant ear plants growing big enough to hide a man standing and the marks of slithering vipers easy to see. They sank their canvas boots into the muck and marched south searching for higher ground, putting their feet on whatever was firmest to leave the least trial. Lizards and dark brown frogs skittered from their path. A cool breeze blew in their faces. The pale yellow brown sky of late afternoon shown over them. Fruitcake's cluck was sharp and clear to them here where the birds no longer *cawed* but whistled. They went to ground. He came back to report. "Stove-in F.O.B. up ahead, Waldo. Looks like ain't been used in couple-three years. Plenty of growth on it."

"We'll skirt it," said Waldo. "You lead out, Fruity, but watch for traps and mines."

They marched in column around the ruined base. It had the look of a Chuck encampment, particularly the shape of the circular mortar pits, and had no G.I. plastic-woven sandbag cover on the overhead logs but sod instead. This had been a big Chuck effort, he had built it for a big fight here in the Valley in the old days. They stared at it in curiosity, wondering who Chuck had fought then.

"Hey, hey!" said Deerslayer on the right flank. He had picked it up automatically and now stood startled at what he held in his hand.

Waldo motioned the column to earth, then approached Deerslayer in a crouch. "That's a mine, 'Slayer."

"I know it. A souvenir of the U.S. Air Force. Can I put it down?"

"You better. Slow." They studied it where it lay on the mushy earth. "Been out here a long while and it's a dud," said Waldo. He and Deerslayer surveyed the ground. "Whole area must be mined." After that battle in which Chuck had used these bunkers, the Air Force had strewn some of its many toys across this piece of valley. It was a weapon suited for comic books: Canisters of aerial mines were dropped to burst open and shower down hundreds of packages that, once the wings had flung open, looked like winged golf balls. The mines glided to earth, struck hard ground, then bounced up into the air head-high and exploded. A wonderful weapon that had no value against men in bunkers, or standing in mud. Of course, there was always a percentage of failures — mines that refused to jump up after striking soft earth. These the Air Force was pleased to leave behind in the Valley, a quick way to mine a large area in a free-fire zone. Unfortunately, most of those mined areas were never properly recorded on operations maps and many American units walked into them.

Mars said, "This could be a blessing. We know Chuck won't come over this way, so if we cut west from here and then head south, we can pretty much count on our left flank being secure for a time."

They marched away from the bunkers and out of the mined area, moving with excessive care and little speed. They cut south-southwest looking for the Chuck trail and the marks showing that Bravo Company was down that way. They feared they may have gambled too much — they could stumble into Chuck or he into them or they could run into Bravo unprepared. The results would be the same.

* * *

As evening began to close around them, Captains Dong and Nguyen brought their units together to discuss what had happened. They had lost

147

all track of the American patrol and that worried them. Either the patrol had flanked them to join Bravo in the south or the patrol had another mission and had gone out east or west. In any case, they had lost contact and they had to report it to higher, higher would be furious. That meant they had to close with the wounded Chuck company in the south that was keeping contact with Bravo and see what kind of a party they could put on in the night to assuage higher's anger over their losing the patrol. Their sixty men plus the twenty-odd leftovers of the wounded company should be enough to overwhelm thirty-three Americans whose ammo had to be running low and who, oddly enough, had called for no Spookies, gunnies or zoomies in the last two days since the fight on Baldy had begun. Bravo must have ruined its radios, a happy bonus for Dong and Nguyen. They moved south in column with point, tail, and flank guards out, not worried about leaving trail – it was their Valley, after all.

* * *

"Hey, Raiby," said Engle, "it's 1800, man. Let's get outta this hole and forget the war."

Raiby rubbed his red eyes. "I believe I'll stick around a bit, Lieutenant."

The night shift came in, its lieutenant saying, "Suit yaself, Rabies. In fact, why don't you hold the fort while we grab some chow from the Airborne Club. Ya want something?"

"Burger, fries, Coke."

"Ya got it." The night lieutenant left.

"You aren't gonna stay here all night, are ya?" asked Engle.

"Just a little longer." Raiby glanced at the radio he had kept tuned to the defunct Bravo freak.

"You know there's nothing going to come out of that radio tonight. We got nothing all day but static. Like I told you, it was leakage from the paratroopers' freaks on Baldy."

"Probably," said Raiby, tapping a grease pencil on the map he had spread out before him on the desk.

"Well, suit yourself," Engle said, shrugging. "See you in the A.M." He left.

Raiby called across to the starched infantry staff officer trading his duty for his own night shift. "Hey, Captain Meese. What say we put a redhaze down there in Valley?"

"To look for Bravo?"

"Never know what we might find."

Meese stared past Raiby at the huge wall map on which they had greased in what little evidence they had that something that wasn't Chuck seemed to be moving through the Valley. The most impressive mark was the artillery fire that had been called in the night before on a Chuck company. It had been an accurate firemission – a company of Chucks had been destroyed, according to official body count. "Yeah, why not?" said Meese, turning to his replacement, a first lieutenant, to give him the instructions.

Raiby had his burger and fries and sat through the first part of the night with the night shift, listening to the crackle from the radios. At 2000 the results of the redhaze were in, the chopper boys wondering why any mission had to be flown that early when everyone knew that Chuckie didn't settle in until after midnight. Midnight for the redhaze — a quick flyover with sensors that could detect campfire heat — and then call in your arty asap just as old Chuck is curling up in his blankets for a peaceful night in his Valley.

The first lieutenant brought the marked-up redhaze chart to Raiby. "Meese says you're interested in this, Sarge. Here you go." He dumped the map on Raiby's desk. Raiby clutched it up and stared at it. "There's a little something down there, all right," said the lieutenant. "Not enough to fire another range and deflection spread. If you want to put some H-and-I in there, you got my approval. No grunt units down that far." He went back to his desk and the crossword puzzle he was working.

Raiby studied the chart. The redhaze had produced enough readings to show a peculiar semicircle of very small camp fires in the forest — about what a G.I. would build in a tin can to cook some rats. But it was a very un-G.I. setup. It looked Chuck, like a Chuck unit worried about taking hits from two sides at once and no time to dig in. That kind of F.O.B. made no sense unless Bravo was down there. And Bravo wasn't supposed to be anywhere. Bravo was supposed to be dead.

He put down the map and rubbed his tired face. He had been with this strange thing so many hours — days now, days following a company he knew had been blown away — that he was no longer sure he was sharp enough or perhaps rational enough to analyze what the redhaze showed. He looked again at the map. All it showed was some stupid Chucks doing something stupid, which was what Chucks did best when they weren't killing Americans. If he missed another evening's poker he could lose another three hundred dollars and lose his seat at the table. He had heard nothing intelligible on the radios in the last forty-eight hours. Perhaps what he had heard in the beginning was, after all, just imagination.

He slapped shut the map, got up, said to the night shift, "See you guys tomorrow," and went up out of the bunker, stretching his arms and legs and arching his tired back to get the cold bunker cramps out of them. He went to his hideyhole to get his gambling money and then down to the N.C.O. Club.

Four hours later and money ahead, Raiby turned up the last card on the dead man's hand — aces and eights, the hand Wild Bill Hickok held at the moment he was shot in the back. Raiby hated that hand, hated seeing a thing another man had seen at the moment he died. He laid the cards face down and folded out of the game to beery shouts of protest from the other players.

He went out into the black cool night and lit a cigarette, feeling a mild breeze drift through his sweaty fatigues. His mind turned to Bravo Company. No, it was always with Bravo. He trudged up the hill to DeeTOC, down the concrete steps into fluorescent haze, and found twenty men staring wide-eyed at his radios. The night shift lieutenant turned to him and said, "Good God, Rabies, someone's fighting a war down in the Valley and no one's supposed to be alive down there!"

* * *

At 2100, when Sergeant Raiby was picking up his first card of the evening and the full blackness of the jungle night had not yet been relieved by a thin line of silver moon, Fruitcake and Spec-Four Lefever, with his basset hound face and the shotgun he despised because he was terrified of its indiscriminate spray of lead, went quietly onto their bellies in the trail muck as the distant muffled roar of an ambush came to them from far downtrail. "I'd say that's a klick south," said Fruitcake.

"About right," said Lefever. A spray of mixed orange and green ricochets darted beyond the treetops. "Bravo."

Waldo and Mars sprang into the mud beside them. "Ya see anything?" demanded Mars.

"Naw. That's a klick farther down," said Lefever.

"Then it ain't the unit we're followin'," said Fruitcake. "That sandal print we spotted was still dry — no time for it to fill with water. They can't be more'n fifteen minutes away from us while that firin' is a good hour's march."

"It's Bravo," said Mars. "They ambushed the unit followin' them."

"Could be other way 'round," said Waldo. He dumped his pack and rifle and, with only his radio on his back, shinnied up the thickest tree at hand. From its top, he could see nothing but black mats of leaves and black sky occasionally streaked with a silent ricochet. He talked into his mike: "Pagan four-six, four-six, this Yonkers two-four, two-four, how do you hear me, over."

Crackles of static. Then the excited voice of Kansas City: "This is four-niner, two-four, never hoped to hear your voice again! Six wants your logger — in the clear, over."

"Estimate one klick due north your logger if you're the boys doing the work tonight, over."

Captain Foley's voice came on line, the racketing of M.G. fire nearly drowning it out: "Your battery's weak, two-four. You got contact with higher or no, over."

"You're our first contact in two days, four-six. Give us your sitrep and we'll be down to help, over."

"We bushwhacked twenty Victor-Charlie dogging our trail and we're pulling out right now. What's yours, over."

"We're dogging estimate fifty V.C./N.V.A. forty-five minutes max away from you coming down from due north on your old trail. You got mortars, over?"

"Rog, mortars. Thanks for the fifty, old buddy. Don't follow me. Do this — call steel if you can, then bug out. You got a map, over?"

"Rog, map."

"Look at it. If I'm Houston and you're Chi-town, then you'll find a big clearing about Albuquerque. We'll meet there, over."

Houston, Chicago, Albuquerque? What kind of map directions were those? Waldo wanted to shout in frustration. They were the only kind Captain Foley ever used, the woodsman who couldn't find his way across a parking lot. Waldo peered at the map he held against his nose, his legs wrapped around the broad tree limb on which he sat, and, nearly smothering the light in the palm of his hand, gazed at the map in the thin beam emitted by his penlight, and found Albuquerque. A clearing was the wrong place to go and Daddy was no map reader but in the midnight jungle full of trigger-happy Chucks no place was safe and any hideyhole was good if it meant joining forces and putting the company back to full strength. "Roger, wilco, over," said Waldo.

"Good, two-four. Call steel and move out now. I'll give you sixty seconds before I drop mortars and run myself, out."

"Roger, out." Waldo flipped over to the arty net and strained his whispered voice into the mike. He was about to give up — despite his treetop elevation and less radio traffic at night, the surrounding mountains were blocking his radio commo — when a voice burst in his ear, saying, "Station calling Yonkers three-one, we can barely hear you, over."

"Three-one, this two-four, two-four, two-four, firemission, over."

"Station calling three-one, I say again, we can barely read, over."

"Two-four, two-four, two-four, firemission, over."

"This three-one. Roger, station, firemission. What is your call sign and logger, over."

"Yonkers two-four, Yonkers two-four. Logger in clear is" — he fought with his map and the tell-tale penlight and spoke the coordinates into the handset.

"Roger, station. We have your logger as..." The voice faded. The radio's battery, unused in forty-eight hours, had consumed just enough revitalized energy to report the useless stuff. Waldo drove his fist into the tree trunk in frustration. His sixty seconds granted by Captain Foley were slipping away.

"This three-one. Attention station calling three-one. Say again your firemission, over."

Waldo clapped the mouthpiece to his lips, speaking as clearly and slowly as possible and as loudly as he dared, knowing voices travel deadly distances at night. "This Yonkers two-four, two-four, firemission, fifty Victor-Charlie, battery-six on this logger" — again he studied his map in the pale, concealed ray of light from the penlight in his cupped hand.

"Roger, station, I have your firemission at" — and F.D.C. repeated the coordinates — "dangerously close to your own logger. Explain and I.D. yourself, over."

"Three-one, two-four, we're buggin' out asaper. Fire when ready, over."

The radio crackled with fresh urgency: "Two-four! Did you say 'two-four,' over." This was a different radio voice.

"Roger, three-one, this two-four, over."

"There is no two-four. You the same two-four called an R-and-D two nights ago, over?" The voice trailed to nothing.

The battery was dead. Nothing to do but hope F.D.C. had enough of the trans to shoot. Waldo shinnied down the tree. "Get Sar'n Mars and the boys," he said to The Bee. "We gotta run for it. Daddy's down south and he's buggin' out due west. He ambushed the unit trailing him." The sudden muted *BANGS!* of Bravo's light 60mm mortars cracked over the trees in the blackness to the south. "He's dropping steel on the forest to cover us. Plus redleg will be here — *here* — in sixty."

They collected the patrol and ran, heedless of noise or trail, running toward a thinning of brush beyond which glowed the fluorescence of horizon cut by mountains.

Noise travels great distances at night, and fifteen minutes below the American patrol the combined units of Dong and Nguyen, on a swift, stealthy, wary plunge south to support the twenty men Bravo had ambushed, heard the patrol's clattering bugout and thought they were being attacked by the American patrol they had been trailing and had lost the night before. They threw themselves down in a circle to open fire in all directions, their green tracers thudding into trees and ricocheting off stone. Foley's light mortars burst yellow up in the treetops and showered them with frags. They groveled in the mud in a black jungle night in the valley that had once been their private preserve.

The clattering of the patrol's hasty bugout saved Chuck lives because the combined units were prone when, three minutes later, the double-racketing, sound-barrier-busting, hideous shriek of American eight-inch howitzer shells came down through the canopy into the spongy earth and tore the forest to bits, men screaming themselves deaf, men flung in pieces into the treetops, sections of steel and stone and spears of tree limbs *whinging,* clattering into the blackness, suddenly erupting yellow, skewering shell-shocked men who were on their feet and running madly as their saner comrades groveled in the steaming shell holes full of jagged bits of hot, muscle-tearing metal. Then it was over.

Waldo had called for a battery-6 — six guns, six times. F.D.C. had given him its only battery of two eight-inch howitzers — the only guns available to range that far into the Valley — but had had the guns fire eighteen times apiece over a modest deflection spread equal to a battery front of six 105mm howitzers.

The Chucks ran fear-maddened, losing equipment and wounded and, once sloshed into a safer place, dug in with their bare hands. The two captains were astonished to count only twelve lost of their combined force of sixty. Of the forty-eight with them, two were wounded, which meant they could count on six more wounded straggling in over the night. They reported only six killed to higher. When higher demanded a better explanation of this new debacle, the captains decided the better part of communication was silence, pretended their radio battery was failing, and clicked off.

They lay there the night in the snake-slithering muck waiting for the next Yank barrage to tear them all to bits, wondering what kind of Yank unit they were trailing, men around them moaning from the pain of the concussions they had suffered, the night eerie and terrifying. Late at night the realization came to them: Nungs! Of course! Chinese mercenaries in American uniforms and equipment. Who else? They hated fighting the Chinese — the mercenaries were animals who took no prisoners, used knives too much, traveled at night and never slept — but that, at least, was a rational explanation they could accept for the weird behavior of this enemy unit. They settled down to wait for predawn, snuggling in their slime, no one sleeping, hallucinating another artillery attack.

* * *

In the fluorescence of DeeTOC the infantry Batco, Colonel Yoden — burly as a football player gone to seed, his close-cropped hair gray, his thick mustache trimmed to within a millimeter of regulation width, his eyes red and yellow with too much concentration on his paperwork — was astounded at the lunacy suddenly hitting him from all sides. He recoiled from the redleg net that Staff Sergeant Raiby had just tuned to catch Waldo's whispered trans to F.D.C., windmilled through the crowd of his suddenly superstitious and imbecilic staff officers, and grabbed a landline, cranking the bells of artillery battalion F.D.C. "Did you just tell somebody you're gonna shoot that mission?" he cried into the phone.

"That's right," came the young voice at the other end of the staticky line.

"On whose authority?"

"My own. I'm the F.D.O. here and it's my job. Who'm I talkin' to?"

"Blueleg Six, who do you think? Gimme your six, kid."

"My six gave me standing orders to shoot whatever two-four might call in, sir. I'm doing it."

"I don't believe that. That's ridiculous. There is no two-four — he got blown away with my Bravo Company."

"Choppers never found his bod, sir, and someone using that call sign and sounding very much like two-four did call in a picture-perfect mission on a Chuck company two nights ago. My six says to shoot for two-four, even if he's Santa Claus."

"I'll talk to your six anyway, kid. Put him on."

"Can't sir, he's not here. He's at L.Z. Action tonight supervising night-fire on Old Baldy for the paras."

"Where's your exec, then?"

"Blown away. I'm it tonight."

"A lieutenant?" croaked Yoden.

"Captain, sir."

"From the Point, I hope."

"Roger. Five years ago."

"Then you must be a good man. Listen to me and be sensible. You can't fire that mission —"

"Is there any blueleg down there I don't have on my charts, sir?"

"None. You know Raiby's too good to let that happen."

"Then I'll shoot it."

"Listen, man, you want to sacrifice the Point and a majority for one stupid mistake? That's what's happening here, you know — I'll burn you so bad in a private memo to the commanding general that no efficiency report your six can write on you — even if your six was Westmoreland himself — will save your career!"

156

The voice at the other end said quietly, "I've got no career, sir. I've got six weeks more in this stinking war and when that's over, I'm out of your army. This wasn't the U.S. Army I wanted to join. It was another U.S. Army."

"You mean you're sacrificing the Point — the Point makes a man a general — for what?"

The line was silent in the Batco's ear. Then the voice said, "Do you know what 'shot, out' means, sir?"

"I do."

"Then: Shot, out."

"You didn't just fire that target?"

Yoden slammed down the handset. "They fired it," he said incredulously. His staff officers cheered. He glared them down. His eyes fell on Raiby for the first time since he'd been called out of his ranch-style bungalow built on the DeeTOC hill to witness the strange hissings from a radio call sign that was supposed to be dead. "Raiby, what the hell are you doing here?"

"Couldn't sleep, Colonel."

"Raiby, you get a goddamn air photo recon mission down there at first light. I want to prove to you idiots that a little static and some bleeding over from other freaks doesn't prove one dumb redleg F.O. is really alive and down there fighting the war all by himself."

"Yes, sir."

The Colonel stomped out of the bunker.

10.

Bravo Company and Waldo's patrol ran out of the forest that was exploding in orange and black from the artillery fire, beelining without noise security for the clearing called Albuquerque. If they hadn't been expecting each other, they would have opened fire on each other. Instead, after thirty minutes of panicked stumbling, with chunks of arty steel shrieking overhead to *thunk* into trees around them, they joined up and then collapsed together in a gasping tangle of waist-high elephant grass, too exhausted to talk, some of them falling asleep immediately.

"Damn good to see you boys!" said the captain between breaths, shaking hands and slapping rumps all around. "Thought we'd lost ya for sure. Did you take any wounded or K.I.A.?"

"None," replied Mars.

"We lost three," said Foley. "We stripped their gear and buried 'em best we could with their dog tags. Hated to do that but we'd no choice. Silva, Skeet, and the Hardluck Kid."

"The Kid," said Pinball. "Well, he was one of 'em never meant to get outta this war alive."

"This is a bad place, Captain," said Waldo. "We got no cover in the open like this."

"I know it. But it was the only landmark I could spot quick in the dark. I figure right now the thing to do is to get into those trees on the south side, circle up, and sack out. Conserving energy's more important than anything else – we're all busted. Then, before dawn, we move due south and keep moving until we're in easy range of the downed chopper before we cut southeast to search for that M.I.A."

"Good plan. But we got some units on our trail."

"You said fifty in the unit you were following?"

"Fifty plus."

"Fifty less," said The Bee, "after all that steel."

"We ambushed a unit of about twenty," said Foley. "We didn't want to do it but had no choice. They acted like they wanted to slow us down for another element to clobber us."

"That's right," said Sar'n Mars. "Those fifty were comin' after you."

"So we can figure on forty to fifty leftovers, then," said Waldo. "What've we got — thirty-one effectives?"

"We gotta find that guy from the chopper and bug out fast," said The Bee.

"If we had to fight Chuck, we could dig in," said Pinball. "Chuck'd need four to five times our number to push us out of a good position. We could dig in and call for help."

"We've got nothin' to call with, Pinball," said Foley. "Waldo, how's your radio?"

"Finished. Battery's dead."

"Well, at least you got that fire in. We got good batts but no radios that'll broadcast more than a klick. Find Kansas City and get his spare batt. Now, we've been here too long. Bee, Pin, Knobs, spread the word — south — now. Sar'n Mars, stay with me. Let's move out."

* * *

Well before false dawn the two Chuck captains rousted their frightened and red-eyed soldiers and led them cautiously into the forest area devastated by the eight-inch guns. It was as though the hand of some hot-blooded Yankee god had crushed down through the jungle canopy, scooped up earth and trees and men, and let it all dribble in ruins between his fingers, leaving heaps of black seeping mud and pits filled with slime and jutting bone.

There had been no wounded straggling in overnight. Nor had there been any cats to stop them — the eight-inch had driven the big cats into their holes. No, the wounded — three of them — had found each other and huddled together against a shattered tree trunk and, together, had bled to death, too much in shock from the bombardment to realize what was happening to them.

False dawn seemed to come up out of the particles of earth. They knew Yank choppers would be there soon to gloat over this victory as they had two days ago when more sudden hellfire had smashed half of Captain Dong's company. They stripped the three dead of material and I.D., threw them into a crater, and buried them. They collected the pieces of the other nine killed and did the same with them.

Then they tramped downtrail to the site of Bravo's ambush to see what had become of the already broken twenty-man company that had been following Bravo. They found ten of them shot to pieces and four more whimpering in the trees. As for the remaining six, they had disappeared. They would eventually show up at headquarters telling lies of heroism. The two captains had the bodies buried and found the common grave of Silva, Skeet, and the Hardluck Kid — stripped, with only one dog tag each — and recovered them. So these weren't Nungs. They were Americans after all. What had gotten into them? Why weren't they acting as they were expected to act?

Dong and Nguyen got the story of Bravo's guerilla ambush of the twenty-man company from the four whimpering survivors, and liked hearing none of it. With the full flush of dawn, they heard the clattering of three choppers overhead — Raiby's photo mission as ordered by Colonel

Yoden — and barreled south into the deeper woods to await whatever fresh disaster their own valley had in mind for them. They were beaten enough to radio the truth to higher, and to beg for help.

* * *

Grunt Batco Colonel Yoden had not slept for his rage. At 0700 he came into DeeTOC red-eyed and angry, furious for two hours until the air-recon photos — eight-by-eighteen black-and-white glossies — were presented to him. "Ah, ha!" he sneered. "Show these to that insolent redleg F.D.O. Sergeant Raiby, get over here! Look at these. Eight-inch can turn over a good two acres of jungle, all right, but there's not a Chuck eyeball in any of it. Ha!"

"Pardon, Colonel," said the photo analyst who had brought the pictures. He tugged a photo from the clump in Yoden's hand and laid it on top. It was the view from a higher altitude showing the target zone and the surrounding canopy. In the thick upper branches of a tree, where an eight-inch round had thrown it, was a man's leg dressed in khaki pantleg and truck-tire Chuck sandal.

"Oh, no," groaned Yoden. It was no longer a bad joke or Raiby's aberration. It was real, whatever that meant in Vietnam. "We got somebody down there in the Valley all by himself, and no way to get him out," said Yoden. He shouted for his maps and his intelligence officer and they went to work piecing together the evidence of the last seventy-two hours, with Raiby as narrator.

There it was, plain on all the maps, on all the back azimuths, on the radio intercepts, on the redhaze — someone was moving south away from Baldy and the first day's battle that had claimed the life of Bravo Company. He was being followed, without doubt, by at least two company-size elements of V.C./N.V.A.. He had called fire on them twice and he had somehow attacked once, perhaps twice, a unit he had found in his path — but attacked with what? How? He had chopped them to bits and he had kept humping south. The evidence was right there to see.

"But, good Christ," said Yoden, clutching the charts, "how can he do all this? Listen, if he's an officer he deserves a Silver Star for this. If he's enlisted, I swear I'll see he gets the Bronze with all the Valor-Vs and oakleaf clusters I can cram on it." He peered at the map. "He's doing great outstanding work. He's single-handedly drawing away from Baldy forces that could be causing the paratroopers extra grief, and they've plenty of that already. It's taken them three days to gain 150 meters and that ain't halfway up the mountain yet." He stared fiercely at the map. "But I don't understand it — how could one guy do all that?"

"May not be just one, sir," said the intelligence captain. "There were two bods missing from Bravo — the F.O. and that buck sergeant, The Bee."

"That's right. Two guys then. But, two guys?"

"Can't be more than that, sir," said the captain. "Two can evade the sniffers, redhaze, photo recons. Any more than that, we'd have seen them right here." He tapped the charts and photos.

The landline clattered and Raiby answered. When he put down the handset, he reported, "Colonel, choppers just back from Baldy to refuel and rearm say they spotted a company-size element moving into heavy canopy two klicks south of Baldy."

"Moving up on the paras, you mean?"

"No, sir. Moving south."

"*South,* Raiby? They *can't* be movin' south. They *wouldn't* be movin' south. The fight's up on the mountain."

"South, they said, sir."

"Choppers take them under fire?"

"Outta ammo."

"Raiby, nobody sends two companies plus after two lost G.I.s. Nobody then sends a third company after two guys when they've got a hell of a fight goin' for them on Baldy." He stared at Raiby, puzzled and furious.

"Yes, sir," said Raiby, "but they would do it if was more than just two guys."

"Now, Sarge," cut in Lieutenant Engle, who preferred to keep his silence in the presence of his Batco, "let's not worry the colonel with your crazy theories."

"Shut up, kid," said Yoden. "What's your crazy theory, Raiby?"

"It's Bravo, sir."

"Who?"

"Bravo's down there. They're after Bravo."

"It would make sense, sir," said the intelligence captain. "They'd send three companies after one company but not after two lone guys."

"Bravo Company of what battalion?" asked the mystified Yoden.

"Of this battalion, sir," said Raiby.

Yoden said, "You two are nuts. Bravo was nuked away. I saw the bods myself. I got a morgue full 'em."

"It's Bravo's F.O. who's calling fire, sir," said Raiby.

"It's on our battalion freak that our radio intercepts have been picking up some strange trans using the Bravo call sign," said the intelligence captain.

Colonel Yoden gazed from Raiby to the captain in fresh fury, but he said with uncharacteristic restraint, "Listen to me. We got us two lost boys down there. They've fallen in with a unit from an A.O. to our south that has gotten off its track and into our territory. They are fighting their way south to their support base. That's the answer. It's the only answer." He slapped the huge map pasted to the wall and said, "In fact, looking at this map you can see if they continue their line of march for two-three days more, they'll be in Phu Bon Area of Ops. Waldo and The Bee have fallen in with some Phu Bon Mike Force. That's all there is to it. Engle," – Lieutenant Engle snapped to attention – "get on the horn to Phu Bon and give me a sitrep asap." Engle ran off to do that. Yoden scowled at Raiby. "When's your R-and-R due, Sergeant?"

"Six weeks, sir."

"Put in your papers this hour, Sergeant. You're leaving today. You need it, bad." The colonel turned to his intelligence captain: "You, Willy, keep out of my sight for a couple days. It'll take me that long to forget my G-2 believes in ghosts. Engle," – Engle snapped to attention with the telephone halfway to his ear – "you may be redleg, but I'm putting a smudge on your efficiency report." He glowered around at his staff officers cowering away from him, shook his head in disbelief, and stomped out of the bunker.

* * *

It had not been an easy decision for the 95-Bravo V.C. regimental commander to send a third company south after those mysterious American guerilla units. Despite the hysteria of the two field commanders — Captains Dong and Nguyen, men he had trusted for cool-headedness but now they had gone mad — there was no disputing the damage these small units had managed to achieve. If all reports were to be believed – and who could really believe field reports from stupid grunts? – the Americans, operating in three tiny independent commands until they linked up last night, had accounted for forty killed, wounded or missing. That was incredible when on Old Baldy – the 95-Bravos had picked up the Yankee name for the mountain – five typically understrength Yank paratroop battalions with gunnies, zoomies, spookies, and plenty of arty had, in three days' battle, cost the 95-B – hastily dug in after Bravo Company had transited the mountain in pursuit of the downed chopper – only fifteen casualties. Against that the 95-Bravos with a boost from the N.V.A. Yellow Division – though they were mostly poorly trained and inexperienced clerks – had wiped out the forty-two men of Bravo Company and, according to radio intercepts and medevac calls, cost the paratroops another six killed and seventeen wounded. It had been a very profitable seventy-two hours for Uncle Ho.

Unfortunately, these victories were all the 95-B could hope for — there were just too many Yanks to make a clean, field-clearing triumph. That was the way it always was, for both sides. It was the basis for the occasionally interrupted peace of the five armies of the highlands. Still, the

commander could have sent the third company sweeping into the paratroops' rear to rack up a better body count. He had sighed when he thought
of the glory of claiming the elimination of, say, another whole company
of Yanks, of paratroopers at that. But he had done the prudent thing, and
the prudent thing was what he always had to do as he was always out-
manned and outgunned — he had sent the third company south after this
mystery guerilla unit. Now, before another twenty-four hours had passed,
he would pull everyone off Old Baldy and leave the barren mountain for
the surprise and amusement of the paratroops. He could imagine the cha-
grin of their battalion commanders when they found their V.C. enemy
suddenly vanished into the forest. How would they write their reports to
their higher to win the glory they wanted? he wondered. The commander
laughed. No, killing Bravo Company would be enough for him. It was
time to withdraw and to write his own reports.

* * *

Bravo Company had made a similar decision and used similar tactics
to get away from the combined units of the two Chuck captains following.
Bravo divided itself into three parts, exfiltrating the woods in which it had
lain the remainder of the night, and then rejoined its parts farther south.
Waldo's was the only radio that could reach basecamp or the somewhat
closer L.Z. Action so they used a fresh battery on it. Though they kept
radio silence to avoid Chuck's triangulating on them, Waldo called in pe-
riodic loggers and sitreps to assure that no errant air cav choppers mistook
Bravo for Chuck. Most of Waldo's commo was with his own F.D.C.,
which accepted that someone who could shoot well was using a dead
man's call sign. So long as he killed Chucks, F.D.C. was not interested in
questioning further. But for fire support coordination and to keep the gunnies off his back, Waldo had to go up to the blueleg net to call Raiby in
DeeTOC.

"Is that really you, two-four, over," Raiby's voice cried in Waldo's ear.

"Of course it's me. You got my coordinates in shackle or not, over."

"Roger, I say 'em back" — Raiby repeated the coded logger. "But, two-four, who's with you — Pagan-four? Over."

"Roger, Pagan-four is here, over."

"*All* of four, over?

"That's a rog, except the wounded you evacked three days ago," said Waldo, growing impatient. "This our plan. From this logger we're headin' azimuth one-eight-five-zero to vicinity new target area I gave you in shackle. Got that, over."

"One-eight-five-zero to target. What's target, over."

"What the hell were we sent down here to find, over," said Waldo in irritation.

"Right on, two-four," exclaimed Raiby. "You mean the chopper? Over."

"Rog. You got new intel on it for us? We figure there's a guy still down there, over."

Raiby's voice was silent.

In his fluorescent bunker, Raiby was wondering what to say — the chopper had crashed four days ago with no survivors and three days ago Bravo Company, sent to its rescue, had as far as the army was concerned ceased to exist. The bones and ash of the three dead that Bravo had recovered were en route to Burgerland for burial. Now Raiby was talking to one of the two missing from Bravo, who claimed he had all of Bravo — call sign Pagan-four — with him and they were going after the chopper again.

Raiby's voice said: "Negative, negative new info, over."

"Rog. Next commo will be when we strike our new logger, out."

* * *

Raiby in his bunker stared at the radio on which a dead man with a dead unit had just signed off. Engle and the intelligence captain stared at Raiby. "Strange what a little static can make you believe, right, Cap?" said Engle.

"Yeah, weird." The captain glanced at Engle's hand still on the land-line. "You talk to Phu Bon A.O.?"

"Just finished," said Engle.

"What did they say?" asked Raiby.

"No Phu Bon units, Mike or other, in our part of the Valley." Engle put down the handset as though he wished he'd never picked it up. "They've also been following the trans of whoever that is down there. Get them lima-charlie, in fact, no static. Trouble is, Phu Bon is an Arvin A.O. so all their radiomen are Viets and speak no English. They hear but not understand."

"There goes the colonel's theory that Waldo and The Bee fell in with some wandering Mikes," said Raiby.

"It was a good theory," said the captain. "What do we give him for a replacement — that Bravo has risen from its body bags and is down there taking revenge on Chuck?"

"We can't say that!" said Engle.

"Hell, no. There's gotta be a more logical explanation," said the cap-tain. "I'm authorizing a sniffer to sweep those coordinates this 'two-four' gave us. If there's a unit down there, we'll smell 'em, count heads, and make eyeball-to-eyeball contact. Engle, you check with Fourth Division to our west and see if maybe their air cav inserted some Beanies on the wrong side of the border. They're always doing stupid stuff like that. Do it now. Until we've got a good explanation for the colonel, we don't let our imaginations run away with us, right, Raiby, Engle? Good." The intelligence officer went out before he risked hearing any more crazy static from the radio.

* * *

Bravo, in its three pieces, moved south. Captain Foley took the center column with Second Platoon led by bowlegged Sergeant Knobs, Fruitcake loping along on point, and the gunman B-2, his eyes now vanished in bruised sacks of worry, as the captain's bodyguard. Corporal Pinball, with the shotgun he feared and hated, would do Foley's map reading for him. They took with them the six walking wounded and Kansas City's radio. There were only three working radios in the company.

On the eastern flank tramped Waldo with The Bee and First Platoon. On the western flank Sar'n Mars, twisting his drooping mustache with his fingers, led the Mortar Platoon augmented with Deerslayer and his big knife.

They were reasonably apportioned and reasonably well armed but low on ammo and food. Water they could always find. Some of them had augmented their poor supplies with what they could hastily steal from the bods of the dead Chucks — they had with them three AK-47 assault rifles, a prize souvenir Chicom pistol, and an N.V.A. bayonet. Ammo for those enemy weapons was low, too: Chuck had carried no more than twenty rounds for each rifle and only two magazines for the pistol. Chuck, too, fought a cut-rate war. They tramped south yearning to fall upon a richly equipped N.V.A. platoon to rob. They dreamed no more of the war's end.

After four hours they had marched five hundred meters, a tremendous accomplishment under steaming triple-canopy where they had chosen not to use machetes but to keep secure silence. Foley leading the middle element called a halt for zonk and grub. Second Plat fell out like marionettes released from their strings, half of them passing out where they fell. Foley gave permission for some quick fires made of C-4 putty in hand-dug pits.

* * *

Although Dong and Nguyen had lighter jungle through which to lead their combined unit, the morning had been a grim one for them, too. They had barely finished their burial chores, cowered away from the heli photo recon mission Raiby had sent out, and crossed the site of the company Bravo had destroyed – collecting the four whimpering leftovers – when a soldier spotted in the mud the prize they all wanted — a souvenir M-16 with a cracked stock — and thoughtlessly picked it up. Of course the Yanks had booby-trapped it with a grenade. The man was killed and two more wounded. They performed another hasty burial and hurried on, wondering how Bravo could make the time in its flight to set the trap. They marched into the first pungi, a sharpened stake stabbed butt-first into the earth, the point disguised by brush and waist high. The first victim died miserably, his body spilling around him as he shrieked like a tortured cat.

Now wary and frightened, they picked their way through the forest realizing that Bravo had had the stakes prepared long in advance and that its rearguard had simply stabbed them into the ground as they ran in case Bravo was followed in their night bugout. Bastards.

Higher was shrieking at them insisting that they pursue the enemy with more dispatch. They shied away from the trail Bravo had left and, keeping one flank in contact with it, moved west. They were surprised to find the morning sun well up over the valley at the moment they plunged from the forest edge and peered across into the empty field where matted grass showed that Bravo had reassembled itself hours before. The radio crackled. Dong answered it expecting to hear more of higher's abuse but he got the news instead that two more radio intercept posts had caught enough of the Raiby-Waldo trans to triangulate a fair fix. He was astonished and unnerved how close the enemy was — almost within eyesight, if the enemy had not marched on swiftly.

Higher had only two commands to accompany this startling news — watch for the third company coming down to help and move due south now to either strike in the flank and hold Bravo for the third company or to get ahead of the enemy and shove it against the third company. Quite reasonable orders, the two captains agreed, if this were a reasonable enemy unit they were following.

They assigned three men to accompany the wounded back to base, leaving them only thirty-nine effectives. They reapportioned weapons and ammo. They led out south, a fresh grimness coming into them all: They had to destroy Bravo Company or Bravo, through some perverseness of the natural order that had once granted the Valley to Chuck, would use the Valley to destroy them.

* * *

L.Z. Action lay at the foot of the grim white bluffs of the Mang Yang Pass beyond which — through the wind-cut gorge 150 meters deep where Highway 19 had been laid — were the 1,000 graves of the dead Frenchmen of Mobile Group 100 who had fought and lost a great battle here just before the final French defeat at Dien Bien Phu. Action was a firebase, home to six 105mm howitzers of Action Battery of Waldo's battalion, the guns laid out in the modified standard format of staggered guns presenting a slightly smaller battery front than the field manuals demanded. The modified front allowed the tubes to be swiveled 360 degrees to fire in any direction and to pump beehive rounds — canisters of thousands of tiny steel arrows — at any enemy close enough to warrant. Half of the firebase was dug into the hard, chalky earth, with rifle slits at ground level. Its distinguishing feature — because a previous firebase commander had been a frustrated engineer — was the thirty-foot tall steel, concrete, and sandbag tower erected by the gunbunnies. The bunnies had hung on the tower their battle flags — California Republic, Dixie, Don't Tread On Me, Spirit of '76, and an assortment of colored bras and panties won in battles in Sin City. But for the battalion commanders, grunt and redleg alike, the tower was not only a lookout but a grand place from which to play General Patton, peering deep into both the Mang Yang through which the convoys sped and into the Valley to the south.

They were there now: The infantry battalion commander, Colonel Yoden with his gray hair, the artillery Batco Lieutenant Colonel Aylward who had authorized his F.D.C. to fire for dead Waldo or anybody else who promised to kill Chucks, and Brigadier General "Mountain" King of the paratroop brigade still slogging its way up Old Baldy and commanding general of this Area of Operations. He was called "Mountain" because, when frustrated in battle, which was too often, he would spread napalm and burn mountains to kill Chucks. His own troops called him "Mad

Mountain." These three commanders were watching the fight on Baldy like it was a silent movie: A this distance, it was lots of flash but no bang.

"Can't believe it," said the general, tapping his manicured nails on his big brass belt buckle with the general's star. "We've been on that mountain four days and we've got only sixty-five confirmed kills. Now you tell me" — he glowered at Colonel Yoden — "that your intel says Chuck is pulling *off* the mountain? Incredible! We haven't hurt him that bad yet." He put a cigarette into his mouth, chewing on the filter as an aide flicked a lighter. "I don't want to leave the mountain until we've got two hundred confirmed K.I.A. I didn't bring five batts down here to walk away without a lot — a *lot* — of kills." He glowered at the Batco. "This op was your idea, Colonel. It's turning into a fiasco. Find a way to stop the seepage of Chucks off my mountain. Find me some kills, not asap but now, hear me?"

"Yes, General." Yoden turned ashen-faced to the paratroop captains there assembled — ragged, dirty, the general had brought these company commanders from the field into L.Z. Action for one of his patented pep talks — and was stunned to realize that of the fourteen company commanders sent onto the mountain, only nine survived. In the five half-strength battalions that composed most of Mountain King's brigade — less than a thousand combat soldiers — the general had taken fifty killed and double that wounded. Fiasco was not the right word for it, disaster was. Without some very creative report writing, or a good V.C. body count, the general was going to get slapped down by his own higher command for this episode, and that meant Yoden was going to lose his command right here. No Legion of Honor. No exit in a blaze of glory. No, in little more than a week Yoden would go home to the hoots of the newspapermen wanting to know why he — the ground commander, not this lofty general — had wasted American lives on Old Baldy, wasted them in a losing war.

That was not the half of it for Colonel Yoden. Back in Burgerland he had a wife, fat and graying, and a child, a daughter. Every time he looked at her, he regretted that she had taken so much from his side of the family:

She was taller than he, over six feet, big-boned enough to be a pro line-backer. There weren't that many men her size to marry her. Yoden had shoved her into college to get her a profession to feed her for the rest of her life. In his neighborhood where everybody knew Yoden by his first name and not as "Colonel," there were other people — young ones, mostly, his daughter's college friends — who hated him for being part of this war and who scorned his undateable, giant daughter for the father's sake. Yoden would rather have killed college students than Chucks to spare his daughter her torment, but he was 10,000 miles from home and helpless. Why hadn't he been smart and politicked for a European assign-ment staring down the Ruskies, and taken his wife and daughter to luxury in Germany? Then slide into an early retirement? No, he had been too smart to be smart. He wanted that general's star on his shoulder. The only way to get that star was to prove himself in war. There was only one war around. He had had to join it. It was the worst mistake of his military life, and there would be no star for compensation, and perhaps no daughter, either. Shame could drive her from him.

"General," said one of the dirty paratroop captains, startling Yoden from his grim reverie, "we've a good idea where the Chucks are drawing off to and suggest we do the same."

"What's that?" demanded the general, chewing the filter of his ciga-rette. King was a nicotine addict but smoked filtered cigarettes. He was not afraid of bullets — in these modern times, generals don't die in combat — but he was terrified of cancer, a more indiscriminate killer.

"For three-four days we've all been intercepting trans from another U.S. unit south of us in the valley."

"What?" goggled Yoden.

"Must be an outfit coming up from Phu Bon A.O. They're kickin' tail down there, sure as hell. We think" — the captain motioned to the other captains — "Chuck is drawing off forces from Baldy, from a fight he can't win, to move south to annihilate this other unit."

"Leapfrog," said the general.

"He wants a little victory if he can't have a big one, General."

173

"What?" Yoden demanded again.

"We let this southern unit draw Chuck off the mountain, Colonel," said the general. "Let them be the lure. Then we use my choppers to extract my troops from Baldy and drop them on Chuck when his back is turned." The general chomped on his cigarette filter. "We soften the target area with gunnies and zoomies and I go home with a victory instead of a disaster."

"But there *is* no American unit down south, General," Yoden blurted out.

"Of course there is."

"We checked it out," said Yoden. "Phu Bon has no one that far north. It's all just freak static. There may be one F.O. and one grunt lost down there from Bravo Company, if the cats didn't get them, but that's it."

General King glared around at his dirty captains. "What've you got to say to that?"

"We stick with it, General. Whoever's down there, Chuck is exfiltrating the mountain to go after him — we've seen high-speed trails he's cut moving south. That unit is drawing him off the mountain."

The general looked into the face of each of his dirty captains and saw the same answer in each of them. He said to Yoden, "If Chuck believes, I believe, Colonel." The general glanced at the horizon. "We've got six more hours of daylight. Colonel, get the choppers and tracks ready for extraction of my troops asap. Ten secs after my boys are out, I want that mountain nuked. Tell the zoomies to spread napalm all over it. We fly my boys into your basecamp, Colonel," he said, calculation in his eye, "until I make my own confirmation of all this activity in the Valley. If it merits, we'll dump my boys on Chuck and eat him alive."

If not, thought Yoden, your troops will be safe in basecamp ready to fly home the same day, leaving me here with the peace of the five armies destroyed, the blood of your fifty dead and of Bravo Company on my hands, my efficiency report wrecked, and my career — what will be left of that? When the newspapers get hold of this, what will her classmates say to my daughter about her father? What will *she* say to me?

* .* *

The 95-Bravo V.C. regimental commander in his tile-walled, electric-lit underground bunker was delighted to have an opponent of the caliber of Brigadier General "Mad Mountain" King. King had come to Vietnam from a different era of war – his version of surprise and maneuver by helicopter gave ample noisy warning to his enemies, enemies who never fought him without the advantage he gave them. The problem was napalm and Kind's love of the stuff.

The regimental commander watched Old Baldy burn with napalm in the clear evening, wondering how he was going to make this disaster look good in his reports to higher: Baldy had represented his safest infiltration route from which to attack road convoys. Built into Baldy over generations of war was an excellent tunnel system, now crushed by Phantoms' bombs and napalm. Inside the mountain the 95-B and the N.V.A. Yellow Division had an advance headquarters and a field hospital prepared, sealed up and ready for use when the time came to make major war. All that now was lost. Worse, despite the unspoken peace of the five armies he now had five battalions of Yank paras flitting over the Valley in their helis, something that had never happened before, and what could that mean for the future of this part of the war?

At least he had extracted his men before the napalm fire came in. The choppers had given him plenty of warning for that. It was not beyond reason that in the near future the 95-B could go back up on Baldy and open up that field hospital and advance headquarters — the paras had not found them because the Phantoms had buried the sealed entrances. But that was tomorrow, not today, when his problems were almost overwhelming.

The regimental commander had one happy advantage: General King, like all his go-go type, was easy to beat. Just give him nothing to fight. Bore him a few days, a week at most. Hope he did not get lucky and stumble over another field hospital dug into another mountain or an arms cache. He would grow tired of inaction and go someplace else looking for easier pickings. The higher they got in the American army, the easier a Yank officer wanted his war. So the commander passed the order — *disappear!* — and the units he had brought down off Baldy seeped into the jungle, into spider holes, caves, tunnels, and were gone.

The commander then prepared his reports in leisure. Radio intercepts told him General King had fifty dead and perhaps three times that number wounded, plus those who had stumbled and fallen getting off the mountain, so the commander reported a healthier 112 Yankee K.I.A. and 250 estimated W.I.A. to higher. How, he thought, to describe the action down south? What could be said about one small Yank outfit that prowled the Valley like Chucks and had destroyed or tied down three V.C. companies? There was nothing to be said that would show credit on the commander. Best leave that out of the report until it could be resolved.

* * *

Foley's voice on the radio said, "All elements, swing southeast on azimuth one-seven hundred. Look to link up at the flanks. We're gettin' close. We'll sweep to the chopper before nightfall and laager there if we must, over."

"Roger, out," said Mars.

"Rog, out," said Waldo. "Let's go, Bee. One-seven hundred toward the chopper and tell the right flank guards to watch for Daddy."

"We gonna make that whole thousand meters tonight? This is light brush but that's a hell of a march even in daylight."

"We got to. Let's move."

They tramped through the forest that was growing blacker as tropic night swept over that corner of Asia. They tramped quickly. Like the moment four days before when they had broken from dreamless deathly sleep on Old Baldy to charge downslope into the fight to save the minesweep tank, they moved with hot determination, careless of fatigue and hunger, with professionalism. They believed themselves unconquerable in pursuit of their mission. This time they would succeed.

All three Bravo elements melded together in the clearing at the base of a small hill, the clearing burned by the falling chopper. Pages of aircraft handbooks showered down on them from the treetops. Sections of light metal that were strewn across the jungle canopy slid and crashed to earth as they chopped through the brush to find the chopper. There it was, as Waldo had found it before — only the tail boom and its one little rotor whole, the rotor cranking over in a light breeze, all the rest of machine and men burned to ash.

Captain Foley, rubbing sweat from his forehead with a black-gloved hand, shouted to the Bravos, "Chuck must know we're here! Circle the area, gentlemen! Set out claymores and pungi stakes. Machinegunners, choose your fields of fire. Waldo, get us some D-Ts plotted. Sar'n Mars," Foley said to him, "get out there and find that last crewman. He's got to be out there alive, got to be. We didn't hike a million miles for another pocketful of bones."

Mars with a search team plunged into the forest.

A voice weak and startled cried, "Hey, hey!" from the trees north of the clearing.

G.I.s ran into the clearing dragging a big man in a ragged flight suit, blood clotted on his face and chest, the man shouting hoarsely, "I'm alive! I'm alive! Hey, hey!"

Foley goggled at the man, rubbing dust from his glasses, then he and Bravo Company swarmed around the man, slapping his back, demanding his name, raising a cheer. Cobb the medic shoved through the crowd to use his last supplies to clean the man's metal-slashed face and bandage his broken wrists. They gave him water, bourbon, tropical chocolate, canned crackers and cheese, the best of everything they had, forcing him to drink and eat, the big man choking with his food and laughing and cheering them and himself. Here, in this moment, Bravo Company believed it had won the war. Not the war against Chuck or against the Department of Procurement or against General Hershey Bar with his conscription list. The war against the things that kill the human spirit.

Mars said, "We better move out, Captain. Been here too long."

"Right. Rog," replied Foley, unwilling to give up savoring this victory. Then he said, "How many grenades we got, Sar'n?"

"Niner."

"Bee, take two of 'em and booby-trap the wreck. All you who were cutting pungi, mount 'em and then saddle up quick. Waldo, plot fire on this logger but tell 'em not to shoot until you say so. You call fire when you hear the boobies blow."

"Saddle up!" said Mars. "Company column. Fruitcake, take the lead. Captain, which way?"

"Due east. I want to get into the mountains and climb out of this filthy Valley quicktime."

"Move out, Fruity. Flank guards! Pinball, you got the rear. Let's go!"

Bravo Company slipped into the forest, moving with speed and care, their fatigue and hunger gone in the flush of their triumph: They had saved the survivor. They had not abandoned him. They had marched across the coals of Hell and they had done it.

11.

Waldo, switching from redleg to blueleg nets as he plunged through the jungle, reported the good news to Raiby for him to pass to higher.

In DeeTOC, Lieutenant Engle gaped at the radio, stunned and frightened. "That can't be! They're all dead!"

Raiby cheered across the bunker: "It's Bravo Company! They're climbin' outta the Valley and they got a survivor from the downed chopper!"

The intelligence captain whooped, throwing his army baseball cap into the air.

The landline jangled. Engle answered. "It's battalion F.D.C. They've got a firemission from two-four and want to know if it's safe to shoot," he said to Raiby out of paled lips.

"There's not another soul down there but Bravo," said Raiby. "Tell 'em to fire."

The blueleg radio crackled with the voice of the Batco: "You got contact down there?" said Colonel Yoden without preliminaries or call signs. "I want to know what the hell's going on — that unit is supposed to be in the morgue, over."

"We already got a sniffer on the way down there, over," replied the intelligence captain.

"Damn right. Out."

The captain shouted across the bunker to a lieutenant: "Get a sniffer over Bravo's logger asap or Yoden will have your butt."

* * *

At L.Z. Action cheers rose from the gunbunnies clustered around the step-down entrance to the battery F.D.C. bunker. In the tower, Brigadier General King stared narrowly at Yoden and the artillery Lieutenant Colonel Aylward. "What do you two mean you've checked it out? You *can't* have checked it out. There *is* a unit down south and if it's not from Phu Bon then it's from Fourth Div or from somewhere else."

"General, it's not Phu Bon or the Fourth, we know that," said Yoden.

"Then who the hell is it?"

The two battalion commanders glanced toward napalm-burning Old Baldy where dozens of slicks were lifting off the paratroopers to return them to basecamp. If Yoden and Aylward could not produce another rich target for King's airborne, King would take them home to his base in the north and blame these local commanders for wasting a big piece of the Department of Procurement's war budget. Vietnam was not going to end happily for the two battalion commanders. "Well, General," said Yoden, Aylward staring at him wondering how Yoden was going to get them out of this mess, "we may not know precisely what unit that is down there —"

"I'm relieved to hear you're not saying it's Bravo Company," said the general.

"— but that unit is doing us a service. Without doubt it's attracting Chucks. It may even be attracting the 95-Bravo elements pulled off Baldy. I suggest we send some of your airborne" — he motioned toward the choppers lifting off the mountain — "down there to meet and greet this unit when it comes up out of the Valley."

The general put another cigarette between his lips, grinding the filter in his teeth. "We know where they're coming out?"

"We can pick a spot and tell them to expect us there."

"They'll want to be extracted," said the general. "They'll want some medals for this. I want photographers." He gazed at the two colonels staring at him. "If we don't pull a good body count on this mish, issuing medals wholesale and writing up this unit's action as our own can get *you* out of the fire."

Yes, us, all three of us, thought Yoden. "That's what I was thinking, General," said Yoden, trying to keep desperation from his voice.

King was being cautious, he was on the verge of winning a paper victory — a very small paper victory with too many American casualties – called "Operation Old Baldy." Or he could throw it all over for one chance with a lost unit that had blundered into a nest of Chucks and make out of that a real fight and a real victory. He said, "We'd surprise hell out of Chuckie if we divert two companies from Baldy and drop them in the south to meet this unit at first light tomorrow, wouldn't we?"

He's talking himself into it, thought Yoden. "That we would, General," he said with bright desperation.

"All right, boys. Show me your intel — redhaze number one — from the past couple hours. Let's get good commo with this unit. Let's see if this is really such a smart idea. We got fifteen minutes to decide, no more. If it's go-go, we divert the next two companies off Baldy and they've got to spend one damn scary night in Chuck's Valley all alone."

The answer was "Go." This operation had started with the sacrifice and annihilation of Bravo Company, gotten too big with the entrance of the paratroops and gotten out of hand with a wasteful, victoryless battle on Old Baldy. No one could afford to let it end with the annihilation of another American unit, unknown and unnamed though it was.

* * *

"We're gonna get outta here!" Kansas City whispered nervously to Captain Foley as they tramped together through the darkening forest. "Higher is sendin' two companies to meet us at these coords" — hands trembling, he gave the captain his notepad — "at first light, and they're bringin' slicks to get us out!"

Foley, puzzling with the coordinates on his map in the fading evening light, was relieved when Kansas tapped his finger on the right place — the eastern side of the mountain range they had begun to climb. He cursed softly, uncharacteristic of the Missouri village parson he was: They had one more unavoidable night in the Valley — no choppers could be expected to come in after dark — and one more mountain range to slog over.

But this time there was someone waiting for them on the far side — two companies of paras. It was true – they were going to make it! "Pass the word," said Foley, folding his map into his front thigh pocket and pushing on uphill.

They had crossed the small foothills into which the chopper had crashed and moved seventy-five meters up the western slope of the mountain range, full darkness all about them and the time on them to slink into the forest to set up their protective circle, when two quick *thuds* came to them thinly through the jungle — The Bee's boobytraps on the wrecked heli. "Chuck's right behind us!" groaned Kansas.

Mars came out of the darkness. "We made only a couple hundred meters max, Captain. The men are bushed and Chuck is too close."

"Rog. This is trail's end for Chuck, Sar'n. Pass the word, Kansas — halt. Take five but everyone cuts three pungi, minimum. We stake this end of the trail, Sar'n Mars, then we cut due south a couple hundred and circle up. Waldo?"

"Here, Captain."

"Chuck is on the wreck. Call your fire now."

"Rog." Waldo clapped his radio handset to ear and mouth.

Overhead, they heard the wild scurrying clatter of the intelligence captain's sniffership as it ran back to base, its pilots terrified at their close call — they'd turned up the thirty-nine V.C./N.V.A. of the combined units, strangely marked by two grenade flashes, and the third company moving south along the ridgeline. The sniffer dived over the mountain ridge into the protection of the two paratroop companies circled-up and dug-in in usual style with a perimeter heavy with machineguns and claymores. Then the sniffer raced past Baldy under the arcing fire of the eight-inch howitzer shells streaking down on the chopper wreck and the combined units.

Bravo Company, its pungi trap set, plunged south into the black jungle.

* * *

It was not the combined units of the two Chuck captains that fell into Bravo's nasty trap on the trail. It was the third company from the N.V.A. Yellow Division, led by Lieutenant Giap, a company of the best available men from the Division's rear elements — battle-trained cooks and clerks. Moving at great speed on ridgetop high-speed trails, depending on the combined units ahead to keep it appraised of trouble, the third company drove its lead elements onto the pungi stakes, the men screaming and writhing as they died, awakening the big cats to howl in their lairs at the moment a great shattering, earth-turning disaster was brought down on the combined units at the chopper by Waldo's artillery fire. Out-flung metal clattered around the N.V.A. company. The once-clear evening air was dense with bitter cordite, dust and atomized blood. Lieutenant Giap turned from the shriekings of his own dying men to see the uphill scrabble of the bloody remnant of the two combined units and himself broke combat silence to shout to them in his Northern accent his warning about the pungi stakes.

Of the thirty-nine effectives in the combined units, twelve — covered with other men's blood and brains, dripping with mud — staggered choking and white-eyed from the black jungle to collapse at the feet of the startled N.V.A. clerks. Captain Dong was among the survivors, the only officer or N.C.O. left alive, tears streaming down his melted face as he thought how close he had come to never again wallowing on his soft, fat wife.

The N.V.A. lieutenant gazed at the 95-Bravos and thought, So these are the much-scorned guerilla-fighters, the men the great Tet battles had destroyed, the men the N.V.A. sacrificed in order to clear them from the political wars to allow more tractable units, more political units, more conventional units of Northerners to have the glory of the great final push against the Yanks to win the war. But he also knew these were the great warriors, and if there was a Yank outfit down there in the Valley's night that could destroy three V.C. companies in four days of running battle, then his motley collection of overage, overweight clerks and cooks had no chance at all.

Lieutenant Giap peered into the suddenly frightening jungle night and ordered his men to slip offtrail and set up a defensive ring in the trees, Nung-style. Then, despite the shame of it, he called the Chuck regimental commander for help.

The 95-Bravo commander received Giap's radio call in the middle of a flurry of surprising and discouraging reports: Not all the paras had been withdrawn from Baldy to basecamp. Two companies had been shuttled south. In the typical noisy confusion of the Yank evacuation of Old Baldy, no one had noticed — or no one had reported — that some choppers flown east toward the Yankee basecamp had ducked behind a mountain range to flit south to insert two companies dangerously close to the units the commander had directed south to deal with the Yank guerilla element. He stared at the decoded message in his hand and wanted to laugh. It was the first time he had seen the Yanks use their own noisy confusion to hide a surprise move. "Mad Mountain" King was going to leave this war with a better combat education than he had brought into it.

Now, on top of that shock, the commander received Lieutenant Giap's report that the two combined units tracking the Yank guerillas had been blown away by more of that hideous artillery fire, and Giap's N.V.A. company — old men who had seen battle too long ago to remember how to do it — was capable of little more than annoying the Yanks. The commander had counted on the N.V.A. only for bodies and bullets. He had expected his own combined units to mastermind and lead the annihilation of the Yanks. Now he was stuck with a major battle in the morning and he was unprepared. He could lose the N.V.A. company, too, and he could not afford to lose it — liaison was already poor with the Yellow Division, and his 95-Bravos needed the Yellow's supply dumps and underground hospitals. Further, he had not done so well on Baldy that he could justify in his reports losing another company — he had already lost three in the Valley.

He began to sweat with anxiety. He cursed himself, the Yanks, the war, Uncle Ho. Three companies utterly destroyed and by what — forty Yanks at most? He wanted to scream. His highers *would* be screaming. He cursed himself for being so stupid as to underestimate a Yank guerilla unit and for having sent forces against it piecemeal. He called up from the south by radio, near the enemy's Phu Bon A.O. where they'd been picnicking, harassing the lazy Mike forces, the nearest Chuck elements — three companies. He ordered them to travel north through the night on high-speed trails protected from sniffers by triple canopy. He ordered them to join Lieutenant Giap's makeshift company on the ridgeline, to sweep west to annihilate the Yank guerillas, and to draw General King's two paratroop companies into the Valley where those three V.C. companies, and more the commander would send in the next day, could destroy the paratroops and allow the commander to bring out of their caves his antiaircraft guns to blow from the skies the five battalions King would surely send to the rescue.

The fight for Old Baldy would be repeated in the Valley. Once again, at King's most frustrating moment, the commander would order the V.C. and N.V.A. elements to disappear into the ground. If he could not beat General King and his limitless armies fed to him from across the sea, he could produce a very fine little battle — to humiliate King and to please his own higher — and a good body count. He was satisfied with that plan. First, however, he had to eliminate this dangerous Yank guerilla unit.

* * *

Giap had done the best he could with the men he had. He had circled them before putting them to bed for the night. They were no better in the forest than were most Yankee units — uncomfortable, suspicious, clumsy, noisy — and they were unfit for a night operation against Bravo Company. He had watched with growing respect as Captain Dong, after the horror of the eight-inch attack, pulled off his ragged clothes, called six others — the only six unwounded V.C. — to do the same, daubed himself with mud and slithered off into the night heavily armed with rifles, knives, grenades, and three satchel charges brought by Giap's company. Dong's team moved south, the only logical direction in which Bravo might have disappeared, to hunt Yanks.

* * *

To the east of the mountain ridge – 170 meters at its highest – on a small, hastily fortified hilltop, the two commanders of the para companies huddled over a foxhole in which a radioman had raised Bravo Company on his radio. "Listen, Pagan-four," the R.T.O. whispered into his handset, "if you hear me, break static twice, over." The two lieutenants huddled closer as the R.T.O. held his handset away from his ear and raised the volume. *Click-click!* "We got 'em, sirs!" said the excited radioman.

"Yeah, and what do we do with 'em?" said First Lieutenant Cassidy to Second Lieutenant Pinch.

"We got a suggestion," said Pinch's field first sergeant accompanied by three more dirty, ragged, half-fought-out N.C.O.s, the shotguns and grenade launchers in their hands dull and black with smoky use. A wretched sliver of moon lit too much of their F.O.B. and lit them. The four N.C.O.s squatted by the hole. "Pardon for sayin' it but higher did us no favors puttin' us on this hill. Come morning, Chuck on those mountains over there can defilade us. If he's got rockets, mortars, or Winchesters, he's got us pinned here."

"We know that, Sarge," said Lieutenant Pinch. "That's why we figure to call air support at dawn and move off this crest onto the ridgeline to meet Bravo as they come over at first light."

"Suggest we move off sooner, like now," said the field first sergeant. "We get ourselves up that ridge and into the trees in the dark, set up, dig in, and get ready for Brother Chuck."

"My God, man," said Cassidy, "you ever march in the dark?"

"On ambush, sir."

"That's a dozen guys. You're talkin' about takin' one-hundred-plus uphill through forest in the dark. Forget it." Cassidy gazed down at the notepad he held in his hand where the coordinates for various sniffer readings had been jotted. There were plenty of Chucks up on that ridgeline — forty, at least — but the sniffer had read nothing that could pass for Bravo, at least not at Bravo's reported laager. Bravo was well dug in or hidden below too-thick canopy to sniff.

The N.C.O.s squatted stubbornly by the foxhole, waiting. Pinch rubbed the stubble on his chin and said, "Cassidy, why the hell you always say 'no' to a good idea first time you hear it and then 'yes' ten minutes later? Say 'yes' now and get it over with."

Said Cassidy, "I don't like this laager either, but Mad Mountain did pick it himself."

"Well, sirs," interrupted the field first sergeant, "it does our morale no good to be pulled off Old Baldy with fifty U.S. K.I.A. and call it a draw. Now we're down here, the boys all been listenin' to Bravo's fightin' for four days, while we slogged up Old Baldy and didn't really hurt Chuck even though we took our hits, and now we're sittin' here like ducks once the sun's up and maybe what Chuck leaves of these Bravos might be just enough to fill one bodybag?"

Cassidy looked over at Pinch and his jaw set. The stubborn man had made up his mind to take another stubborn road. "Whatdya say we give Chuckie a little technical warfare, Pinch? These sniffers are just thirty minutes old so we know what's out there but Chuck doesn't. What say we call for sniffers and redhaze every hour and use 'em for guidance as we climb the ridge? We call a little arty to keep Chuck awake and make the little bugger red-eyed in the mornin'. When Bravo gets up the ridge, we're sittin' on top, dug in, ready to send out a couple of reinforced plats to lead 'em home. Eh?"

"A nice conservative approach," said Pinch. "Just what I woulda expected from you, Cassidy."

"I like it, too," said the stolid field first.

The first of Captain Dong's grenades went off on the western slope of the ridge, near Bravo, its report a muffled *bang!*

"Yeah," said Pinch, scraping the itchy stubble on his jowl. "You," he said to Cassidy's R.T.O. in the foxhole, "tell Bravo we're comin' up the hill and we'll meet 'em on the top at dawn. Get three clicks for reply. Let's go."

The paras slipped off their hilltop and were gone as the sliver of moon sank beyond the Earth, the Chuck observers in the hills around blinking in surprise at what they thought they had seen, but then discounting it — after all, Yanks never marched at night — and reporting nothing to higher. They passed a safe and peaceful night watching an empty hill.

* * *

The grenade flung by Captain Dong bounced off a tree trunk and burst. Fragments pricked and burned the G.I.s lying within fingertip reach in their circle, the brief yellow light of the burst showing Dong nothing — the Yanks were prone and well camouflaged. Nor did they open fire in reply. Good discipline, he thought, but he knew of no Yankee unit that could stand the battering he was going to give Bravo and not either run or fire into the two machineguns Dong had brought from the N.V.A. company. These Americans had a lot to answer for, not the least that excellently vicious trap they had set for Dong and Nguyen at the downed chopper, the trap that had made Dong see more clearly than at any other moment in the war that all the things he most loved but especially his soft, fat wife could be taken from him in an instant by impersonal unexpected steel from some distant gun called on him by some equally coldhearted Yank hiding behind a tree. Dong would score some revenge kills tonight to hold Bravo here for the three Chuck companies humping up from Phu Bon. Most of all he would have the special satisfaction of murdering the men who had murdered his company.

He sent a man forward with a pistol wrapped in a piece of cloth to hide the flash, then sent two more slithering in the opposite direction to help determine the size and fortification of the enemy unit. He waited a half hour for them to get into place and to choose targets, then he hurled another grenade and, in its burst, the pistol man fired once and the others with rifles opened fire. There was a single prolonged agonized scream and no returning orange tracer fire from the Americans. The trick hadn't worked.

Dong lay unmoving for an hour, listening for sounds that would betray Yank movement, one of the three satchel charges in his hand. He was startled at the first distant burst of incoming artillery fire. Two rounds. Harassment and interdiction fire only, from the paratroopers on the other side of the ridgeline. He ignored it. During that hour, one of his men on the far side of the American position hurled in another grenade and his men in two other locations fired bursts of automatic rifle fire. But to none of that did the Yanks reply. Their fire discipline was manic. He would have to stir them up with his satchel charge.

He began to crawl forward. There, jutting from a tree trunk at a ridiculous angle for a branch, was a long straight shadow. Dong wanted to cry out! It was a man standing there with a spear in his hand ready to pin him! The man fell forward, bloody foam spattering on the captain, the pungi spear driven through his chest still clutched in his hands with the blood-soaked, cloth-covered pistol. Dong rolled away from him. One orange tracer zipped into the earth by the dead man. Dong loosed at the enemy flash a green burst from his AK-47 and rolled away again. There was no return fire.

He began to sweat, wiping the jungle slime and salt sweat from his face. Another hideous scream! As though a big cat were clawing apart one of his men, and it *was* one of his men — he screamed for his mother in Vietnamese before his wail was choked off.

All right, thought Dong, I've lost two but I can't crawl back to an N.V.A. company of clerks and cooks to tell them I was frightened away. He slithered forward, the satchel charge slung over his back, taking a long hour to crawl twenty meters through the spongy jungle floor of vines, snakes, and startled little night creatures daring to skitter from their holes in the long silence since the screaming stopped. Far away and muffled through the jungle were the occasional bursts of harassing artillery fire directed by the paratroops.

He heard at last the soft scrape of leaves on fabric as a man wearing pants shifted position. Dong was within a body's length of the enemy line. He took long minutes to draw the satchel charge from his back, to put his hands on the fuse, to study the blackness around him looking for clues to his target. Ahead, he thought, and to the right. If he was close enough to hear a man shift his legs, he was close enough to throw the satchel into the very center of their position.

He glanced to his left and noted a thick tree root system rising from the base of a broad tree. That would give him all the protection from the charge that he would need. He studied it long minutes to be sure there was no one else in there among the roots, then he pulled the rasping fuse on the charge. The Americans had been waiting for him! The muzzle flashes of three rifles exploded in his face — one round each rifle, good fire discipline — but he had hurled the satchel and was already rolling under the brush toward the thick roots. He heard the satchel strike the spongy earth in the enemy position and suddenly it erupted and there was screaming and bits of flying wood. He had rolled bumping into the huge root, trying to control his excited breathing so not to give himself away. He saw the Yank's face. The man half rose from his lair beneath the tree and with a single flash of blue metal slit the screaming Captain Dong from belly to throat.

Deerslayer rolled away, wiping on the earth the mess from his bowie knife, the screams of his buddies gradually muffled behind him.

A burst of green tracer spattered across Bravo's circle, their position defined by the satchel charge burst, and one impatient burst of orange replied, flinging the Chuck rifleman into the forest.

Bravo's defensive circle shrank. They stripped the dead of weapons, ammo, water, food and left them where they lay. The wounded they shoved into the center of the circle as they edged backward until the circle of soldiers touching fingertips was again unbroken. It was now that the flyboy they had saved, the symbol of their triumph, with his broken wrists, groaned out of his sleep, and they realized they had one more task to accomplish.

They roused him awake, the delirious survivor of the downed chopper. He gawked at them unwilling to believe in them, frightened more of them than of Chuck. But the ghost soldiers came to him one at a time, Captain Daddy first, and touched him: Sar'n Mars and Waldo, The Bee, Peepsite, Fruitcake, Pinball, Knobs, Deerslayer, Ayrab and the others. They said to him, *Our part is almost done, buddy, but you have one more hike to make. In every battle of truth with falsehood, there is always one chosen to live to tell the tale. You are it. Tell them of us, tell America.*

The survivor lay conscious in the center of the circle, staring up at black night, stunned by his new responsibility. The Bravos lay through the last hours of darkness, trading clicks on the radio with the para companies coming up the mountain to meet them at first light. This night for the Bravos there were no reveries of the war's end. The war would never end.

* * *

False dawn seeped into the jungle. Captain Foley, Waldo and Sar'n Mars moved crouching through their little F.O.B. They gazed upslope through the trees and yearned to be up on that ridge now with the para companies. They checked the chopper survivor to assure that he was well enough to march despite his broken wrists — he was infected, delirious, silent, staring at them with unblinking eyes. Bravo Company rose quietly

191

from the seeping earth and slipped uphill through the trees, gathering what weapons they could from the corpses of Captain Dong and his men, delighted to find one of his two machineguns unbroken and two AK-47s, giving three clicks on their radio to the paras as warning.

The morning silence was oppressive. The distant *krump* of incoming artillery fire directed by the paras was gone. Not a bird sang, no brushbuck barked. No signs of slithering snakes or prints of cats to prove that any creature but Chuck had moved in the Valley in that grim night. They tramped in silence, using no machetes, slowed by the staggering pace of their wounded survivor and by their refusal to cut trail. They crouched uphill, staring around for Chuck, a weary, bloody, battered crew.

The forest thinned as they climbed, the triple-canopy disappeared. With the first full flash of morning, they looked up through the branches to see there on the slope above them a radiant splash of sun playing on the two companies of paratroopers swinging over the ridge top coming down for *them!* There in the east, leaping up black and slick against the brassy morning sky, were six Cobras and a long stick of slicks. They were going to make it!

They burst through the trees running upslope — only one hundred meters to the paras — gasping and stumbling, and they charged into the startled faces of the three Chuck companies that had hastily set up on the ridgeline. A blaze of fire roared out of the enemy trees. Sar'n Mars thought he shouted, "Charge the guns!" but his head exploded. Captain Foley was blasted flipping downslope into the trees. But Bravo would not be denied – it had its survivor and its triumph – and ran screaming into the enemy line. Waldo and The Bee were among the Chuck companies and shooting down the length of the Chuck ambush line. The survivor ran past them and through the Chucks, running for the protection of the paratroops above them on the slope. The paratroopers shouted their battlecry and ran down into the Chuck rear. Gunships swooped down on the flanks chopping at the Chuck companies. N.V.A. Lieutenant Giap burst out of the trees leading his company of cooks and clerks in a flank attack. And it was done. Done! Bravo was blasted away to atoms before the eyes of the paratroopers and the Chucks. That great internal engine that drives a man to soldier for a dream letting them vanish into death, at last.

Afterword

Old soldiers from that war ask three questions before they accept you as a true comrade of their war: *When were you there? Where were you? Who were you with?*

The question "when" asks to know if you were there in the 1950s when the enemy was armed with crossbows and a U.S. soldier wore khakis and gleaming brass in the field. Or were you there in the half-million man year in the late '60s when nothing gleamed except the enemy's green tracer fire?

The "where" question asks to know if you slogged through Delta mud booby-trapped with infected pungi stakes or if you were at Khe Sanh running from blown bunker to bunker to save your life or were you in the Highlands in that two minute break in the war when they were sleepy?

"Who" asks your unit. Were you a helicopter cowboy or a grunt groveling in his foxhole in a unit that was brave – not just courageous and steadfast, as all Army units must be, but *brave* in the old soldier's understanding of the word.

I reply with all an old soldier needs to know about me: '68-69, Walker A.O., 2/17 Artillery.

For more about my books, please check out these websites:

https://www.stevenhardesty.com
https://www.stevensandmarlinbooks.com

Vietnam War Novels
Ghost Soldiers

War Lover
Saigon Blues
Poisoned Hearts
The Heart Attack (short story)

Dirty Wars Novels
The Runaway Man
Soldiers of Misfortune
The Killing Hour

Westerns
The Gunfighter
The Outlaw
The Bountyhunter
Broken Spur

Crime Capers
The Feathered Virgin
The Dimpled Python
The Laughing Camel
The Elephant Dance
The Flying Pig
The Lazy Tiger
The Cracker Kingdom

More Novels
In the Season of Poison
An Earthman Born
Running in Heels

Civil War History
Confederate Origins of Union Victory

Made in the USA
Las Vegas, NV
06 September 2022

54727562R00121